I, a living arrow

Young
South African Writing 2

Compiled by
Linda Rode and Hans Bodenstein

KWELA BOOKS

Contributions originally written in Afrikaans and those in isiXhosa
were translated by Maren Bodenstein and
Iolanda Oosthuizen

The photograph used on the cover was taken by Andrew Putter
at the 'Deep Space' interschool costume-party
held at Rondebosch Boys' High (with Rustenburg Girls' High and Westerford High School)
in April 1996. All decor and costumes were made by students

The title 'I, a living arrow'
is borrowed from the similarly titled contribution
by Jodi Rosenberg

Copyright © 1998 Kwela Books
Broadway Centre 211, Foreshore, Cape Town;
P.O. Box 6525, Roggebaai 8012

All rights reserved
No part of this book may be reproduced or transmitted
in any form or by any means, electronic, electrostatic, magnetic
tape or mechanical, including photocopying,
recording, or by any information storage and retrieval system,
without written permission of the publisher

Cover design and typography by Nazli Jacobs
Set in 11 on 13pt Plantin on DTP
Printed and bound by National Book Printers,
Drukkery Street, Goodwood, Western Cape
First edition, first printing 1998

ISBN 0-7957-0073-3

Dedicated to
those young people who dare to
tell the truth

Acknowledgements

The compilers and publisher wish to express their sincere thanks to:

Sanlam
for its indispensible financial support

the many language teachers who cooperated by entering their students'
writings

as well as
Andrew Putter of Rondebosch Boys' High School
Jill Joubert of the Frank Joubert Art Centre, Newlands
Leon Büchner, subject advisor: Art at the Western Cape Education Department
Liesl Hartman of Battswood Art Centre, Grassy Park –
all of whom provided students' artwork and
kindly gave permission for it to be reproduced
in this publication

Contents

List of artworks
Foreword
"Home thoughts from abroad" – *Suzanne Cox*, 17
A portrait of '97 – *Ilan Chait*, 19
Market-day – *Tamarra Subramony*, 20
A salute – *Nokukhanya Ngobese*, 24
My masked rage – *William Phillips*, 25
Barman – *Jaco Ferreira*, 26
Child of the pavement – *Emmerentia Erasmus*, 29
Undulukil' uSlovo – Slovo has departed – *Jeffrey Brilliant Tyesi*, 30
Hope is lost – *Deshandra Dass*, 31
The tin cup – *Heidi Swart*, 32
The professional Bushman – *Anya Subotzky*, 36
Earth to mankind – *Megan Jones*, 38
Woodstock Cave – *Philip Samuel*, 39
Checkmate – *Lenelle Foster*, 40
Mara – *Anica Bester*, 44
Think before you leap – *André Kritzinger*, 47
You have so much more – *Nili Dahan*, 50
I, a living arrow – *Jodi Rosenberg*, 51
Pink-Roses Panado – *Cecile de Vries*, 52
A six-year-old doesn't know – *Debbie Berman*, 55
The beginning – *Marcelle Olivier*, 57
Do you also see the red flower? – *Nicolette Maartens*, 58
Peace – *Jeffrey Brilliant Tyesi*, 62
The passage of life – *John Vorster*, 63
The meal – *Pieter Vermaak*, 66
The Romany Creams – *Petro Faasen*, 67
A banquet for two – *Ansulie du Preez*, 71

Be gentle on my mind – *Ilan Chait*, 72
A prison for my soul – *Rachel Grace van Vuuren*, 74
Misty water-coloured memories – *Sanel van Wyk*, 77
The interview – *Brandon Horwitz*, 79
Wallflowers – *Joanne Hobbs*, 82
Only sixteen – *Thomas Cox*, 85
Locked away – *Liron Meister*, 87
These things happen – *Julia Smuts Louw*, 88
On my way home – *Ivor Petersen*, 89
Chains – *Sharon Radebe*, 90
Self-portrait – *Danielle Levin*, 92
The telephone conversation – *Renél Espag*, 94
Mr Hangman – *Louise Crouse*, 95
The thirteen steps – *Ezanne Jordaan*, 98
Where the roads fork – *Adèle Goligorsky*, 99
In the dead of night – *Novuyo Halimana*, 103
The adventures of a wild Afrikaner-wannabe – *Michelle Matthews*, 105
The more-green leaf – *William Phillips*, 109
Though I hear your call – *Shira Hockman*, 110
Moment of terror – *Sanjesh Philip*, 111
To risk – *Nolusindiso Mali*, 115
"Summertime and the living is easy" – *Graham Thurman*, 116
Compassion – *Clare Matthews*, 118
A handful of rain – *Barend Lintvelt*, 119

List of artworks

Linocut – *Michelle Woodman*, title page
Monotype – *Robin Brooks*, 18
Photograph: Social documentary – *Denver Hendricks*, 23
Duo-tone linocut – *Keith Kila*, 28
Photograph: Still life – *Isabel Carstens*, 33
Mixed media drawing – *Karl Mostert*, 39
Pencil drawing – *Talitha Kotzé*, 45
Contour line-drawing – *Nadia Price*, 49
Linocut – *Sindile Ngamlana*, 54
Collotype – *Christopher Wadely*, 59
Photographs: CD-cover design – *Brendon Bentley*, 65
Monotype – *Natalie Nicholas*, 70
Linocut – *Igsaan Barendse*, 76
Cut-out collage – *Waleed Hendricks*, 81
Mixed media drawing – *Thando Koda*, 86
Contour line-drawing – *Andrea Gordon*, 93
X-ray etching – *Camilla Fraser*, 97
Cut-out collage – *Fatima Khan*, 102
Collage – *Denton Isaacs*, 108
Photograph: Still life – *Amelia Kühn*, 114
Water-colour sketches – *Andrew Jamieson, Macieck Strychalski, Taariq Nordien, Rupert Jeffries*, 117

Foreword

This collection of prose, poetry and excerpts from the work of students in their final two years of high school is the second in the series "Young South African Writing". Kwela's decision to publish forthcoming editions in at least two South African languages was inspired by the interest created by the first collection in 1996.

With *I, a living arrow* this intention has been realised, and the compilation is available in both English and Afrikaans, the reason being that more or less equal numbers of entries were received in these two languages; in addition, a few contributions were submitted isiXhosa.

In this collection, the quality of the entries is once again high and the themes and perspectives are diverse, informative and colourful. Stylistically, too, the contributions give proof of amazing creativity and a courage to experiment.

How acutely relevant to our South African society the themes are, whilst universal at the same time, is illustrated by texts such as "Only sixteen", a harrowing piece on drugs and teenage suicide; "I, a living arrow", the title-story, which sketches the sad lack of understanding between a mother and her daughter; "Barman", about the shattering situation of having no work and no future; "Misty water-coloured memories", inspired by the trauma of child-abuse, and "Though I hear your call", the surreal description of someone who cannot step out of her circle of isolation.

Uniquely South African as well as universal are the more optimistic pieces like "Undulukil' u Slovo", a praise song to a deceased hero of the struggle; "A handful of rain", an "ode" to the joy of young love and togetherness – whilst "'Summertime and the living is easy'" celebrates the unbridled exuberance experienced at the onset of the school holidays.

However, the cautious, almost euphoric spirit of political and social optimism of two years ago has made way for a distinct and general feeling of disappointment, of being stuck in a world of increasing violence and growing alienation. What is striking in numerous submissions is the seeming lack of forgiveness, tolerance and mutual understanding between historically opposing groups.

Another interesting aspect of this year's crop is the high frequency of what can be called mini-thrillers. Could it be the influence of the graphic novel and Gothic-horror magazines? Or could it perhaps reflect a subconscious way of trying to cope with the current phenomenon in our society of criminality and violent death?

The truly interested reader will probably conclude that the contributions in this collection are typical of a society midway in the painful process of healing itself, while new wounds continue to be inflicted.

The importance of offering young people the opportunity "to tell the truth" as they see and experience it is underlined by what Aristotle said about writing: it brings to the surface our pent-up subconscious emotions and thoughts, opens up wounds, drains them and exposes them to fresh air. This painful process, known as catharsis in Ancient Greece, is one of cleansing and healing.

Although *I, a living arrow* records the spirit of a specific moment in South Africa's history, it will hopefully also contribute to the healing of our society.

We are thankful to Sanlam for realising the importance of creative writing in our schools and the need to stimulate critical thought by projects such as this. We gratefully acknowledge their financial support. A third edition in Kwela's "Young South African Writing" series is planned for 2000. We hope that it, too, will contribute towards restoring forgiveness, tolerance and mutual understanding.

The compilers
Cape Town, May 1998

This is the world.
Have faith.

Dylan Thomas

"Home thoughts from abroad"
Suzanne Cox

There is a voice within me
that calls longingly for my home,
the country I hardly know.
It's the voice of my people
calling to me,
singing the songs of South Africa,
their homeland – and mine.

This homeland,
this place of my birth,
this home of my ancestors,
calls me back
like the moon pulls the tide.
(fragment)

> Written by Suzanne Cox who grew up in
> South Africa but completed her schooling in Canada

Robin Brooks – Battswood Art Centre

A portrait of '97
Ilan Chait

Clunk-lock. Doors are secure. Cell transfer for prisoner CHA 567. Cross-check. Left bushes, blindspot, right bushes. All clear. Proceed cautiously.

I travel down your gun-barrelled highways and along your concrete vistas. The prison capital. With each house another damp cell. Your railway tracks: ugly varicose veins squeezing your plasma along. A swollen, diseased mass of blocked arteries and a heart that's pumping its last. Shame, if only you had looked after yourself when you were young.

A chilly whiff of diesel fills my nostrils as, no more than two metres inside the barbed-wire sanctuary, I stop. Request for valid identification and authentication. Genuine white tag verified, I may proceed.

In some ways, South Africa, I think I should be thanking you. For you are a true mother. Grooming has started in the home and by the time I leave your training grounds, I will be the best prepared and most alert young man this land has ever seen. All senses fully developed, the finest reflexes, the ultimate edge.

Above all, you have taught me manners. Why, if someone should request anything of me, I shall gladly hand it over without a thought, for that is the right and only thing to do. Not to comply is surely punishable by death.

Were it not for you, we would all be careless clots, not looking left or right before we cross, not to mention back and front. A free, contented nation. A people with no daily excitement.

But "free" seems to be your middle name, mother: a nation not separated by race, colour or creed. And look at what you have already achieved. Look at your children today. Nothing but a bunch of happy inmates – in a rather large John Vorster Square.

Grade 11 – *King David High, Linden, Jhb*

Market-day

Tamarra Subramony

"Out of the way, Uncle!"

Aramugan Pillay was violently flung aside as two small brown streaks raced past him in pursuit of a ball. The handles of his flimsy blue plastic packet gave way to the weight of a kilogram of tomatoes and onions. Aramugan stared abjectly as the vegetables spilled and bounced crazily over the gravel floor of the Durban Squatters' Market. No one else seemed to have noticed.

A self-assured pair of high heels stepped warily over an onion while a tomato was squashed vengefully by a pair of takkies trailing behind. A stream of expletives squirted from the lips of their teenage owner. With mingled fascination and horror Aramugan Pillay watched the tomato juice create swirls of colour as it merged with other smears of dubious origin. And he recalled a similar incident, many years ago, when he was still a boy.

"Ama, look, your new red sari is messed with mud."

"Hush, Aru," Mrs Pillay had said, bending down to pick up the vegetables which had spilled from the torn brown paper bag in the old Zulu man's hands.

The old man bent over and grinned at Aru. "You're looking after your Ama nicely, eh naina?" His wrinkled skin reminded Aru of the hippos he had seen in the Umlaas River nestling in Zeekoe Valley, the home of so many Indian market gardeners. Aramugan took one peek at the toothless gums and clung to his mother in terror.

Mrs Pillay straightened her back slowly, handing the last onion with a mud-splattered hand to the man. He thanked her profusely and limped away.

"Ama?"

"What is it now, Aru?"

"Why did you pick up those vegetables, Ama?"

Mrs Pillay stopped and placed her hand on her son's arm as she always did when she had something serious to tell him. "Aramugan, we must always treat old people with respect, whether they are of our own people or not. This is a law of life." Her hand on his arm grew heavier.

A woman's voice brought Aramugan back to the present. "Are you all right, sir?"

"Huh?" Aramugan blinked several times, his throbbing mind shifting painfully to the present. The sheet of blue plastic which filled his field of vision, slowly materialised into a bag of vegetables dangling before him. He stretched out his hand to accept the bag. As if in a dream, he watched his hand descend on dark flesh. Too dark. Aramugan recoiled.

"These are your vegetables, sir."

The neatly dressed, elderly African woman stood above him with bowed head and a straight face. Aramugan thought he saw suppressed amusement and mockery in the composed expression and bowed head. Gingerly, he took the bag from her. With a glare that belied his muttered "Thank you", he limped away with all the dignity he could muster.

Back home in the bathroom the soap slipped through his fingers as he rubbed them together vigorously for the third time. He opened the tap and let the cold water rinse away the last of the lather. He dried his hands roughly, trying to vent some of his rage.

"How dared she? Nobody asked her to touch my vegetables. You can't turn your back for a moment these days without one of these Blacks trying to steal from you."

Aramugan glared at the bag of vegetables lying untouched on the kitchen sink. He couldn't eat them now.

The words of Sanjay, his son, sprang to his mind: "You're full of these silly, unfounded prejudices, Dad. When will you realise that we are all just human beings?" Aramugan jerked away angrily, struggling to drown the old surge of pleasure and pride which he used to feel when he thought of his only child. He remembered with pain the euphoria which he and Ambigay had felt the day when Sanjay had said he would bring his fiancée home to introduce her to his parents. And then he had dared step over the threshold of his parents' home with a black woman on his arm!

"Where is your fiancée?" Aramugan had asked, refusing to register what he saw.

"Ha! Always the kidder, my dad!" Sanjay had explained to the woman. "Meet Nandi, Dad."

Nandi! The holy name of Lord Siva's sacred cow!

It had required all Aramugan's emotional strength to prevent himself from slamming the door in their faces. Then he had left with a hastily concocted story about an urgent appointment. Later he informed his son that all his ties with him would be cut if he did not break up with the woman immediately. Sanjay, a typically stubborn Pillay, refused.

Aramugan thought of the many changes he and Ambigay had survived – even the loss of their prize farm in Zeekoe Valley to the Durban Corporation to make way for the sprawling Chatsworth township, had not crushed them. But Ambigay's will to live had died on the day they lost Sanjay. And with Ambigay's death all hope for a reconciliation between father and son was lost. So Aramugan continued living alone in his little house in Unit 2, Chatsworth.

He viewed with contempt the transition to a new South Africa and clung desperately to the belief that Indians were a superior race – despite the fact that Sanjay and Nandi had angelic children. Despite the kindness shown to him by an unknown black woman, while fellow-Indians had trodden on his food.

Aramugan wept. He was afraid that the amusement in the woman's eyes had suggested superiority.

The next morning, just when the dark was beginning to fade, Aramugan mopped up the last of the tomato and chutney on his plate with a chunk of brown bread. He washed the plate, glancing out of the corner of his eye at the plastic bag with its now diminished contents. Then, lifting the large pumpkin which he had been saving for the winter, he began the journey back to Durban.

Ripples of sunlight played on his thin figure as he entered the market-place. He went to where he knew he would find her. "Excuse me, ma'am," Aramugan said with excruciating slowness.

The African woman turned round with questioning eyebrows.

Aramugan held out the pumpkin. "This is for you as a token of my gratefulness for your help yesterday."

Embarrassed, he quickly spun around and began walking away.

"Wait!"

Aramugan froze in surprise. The woman's face broke into a broad smile. "How would you like to share this with me for lunch at my fire, sir?"

Something broke deep down in Aramugan. Tears rolled over his cheeks.

"I would love to."

Grade 12 – *Dr A D Lazarus Secondary, Durban*

Denver Hendricks – Frank Joubert Art Centre

A salute
Nokukhanya Ngobese

Our dead heroes I salute:
Steve Biko, Chris Hani, Oliver Tambo,
Joe kaSlovo, Harry "The Lion" Gwala.

We hear:
    The storms of prejudice are passing
    The floods of hate and apartheid will recede
    The reign by detention is broken
    The wailing of women and children will cease.

We see:
    Blood is still shed
    Innocent victims are killed
    Slaughtered human flesh still stinks.

We should be rejoicing
We should be dancing
We should be happy
    But are we really free?
    Is it freedom that we hold in our hands?

To you people, who say we are free,
That's a lie that you tell.
How can you be free
If you encourage destruction
And not reconstruction of the young?

The AKs you've held so close to your bodies
With the evil spirits within you!
Who do you think feels free in your company
While your eyes are filled with anger and hatred,
Your nostrils blow blue, invisible flames?
You traitors! You say you have brought us freedom!
What a green lie you preach.
Ubuntu? You don't have *ubuntu* within yourselves!

Our heroes dead and living
Will not be disgraced and insulted by you.
Come, Africa! Salute your heroes:
Steve Biko, Chris kaHani, Oliver Tambo-o-oo.
Salute Nelson Tata Madiba!
(shortened)

      Grade 11 – *Sacred Heart Secondary School, Verulam*

My masked rage
William Phillips

Share the rage behind my smiles
See the despair in the tears I do not shed
I stand with polished boots
Convicted without trial
I live on paper
Yet you who judge
Sentence me to death
(fragment)

      Grade 11 – *St Stithians, Randburg*

Barman

Jaco Ferreira

I am white. I was born like that. My mother is white and my father is white. Both my grandmothers are white, and my grandfathers. My entire family is white. Even my dog! I have darkish hair. My eyes are nearly black too ... but my face is plain WHITE!

Today I got a form from the university. They won't give me a bursary. Dad will be angry. He does not have any money. I took the form and threw it into the rubbish bin. After a while I took it out again and put it into the ashtray in the lounge and burnt it. It was a mistake! The air stinks. When Dad comes home I will have to confess why the picture of the white barman in the ashtray is suddenly black. It's funny. After the paper had burnt there was no white left, not even a small bit. Just black.

When Dad comes home he will want to know. One day, I will have to tell him about the form! It's not so bad if I don't go to varsity. I will get work: a job. One of my friends was looking for a holiday job. He doesn't have money either. Some places said no. Ster Kinekor, Edgars, Spar. Pick 'n Pay took his name and number, just in case. He is still waiting for them to phone him.

Dad will be home just now. I'll hear his old wreck immediately. It won't even help to try to blow the smoke away with the fan. The lounge still stinks. Mom will also throw a scene. There is so little she can throw a scene about, so she looks for every opportunity. "Ma, I accidentally ..." I don't know what I will say to her. It doesn't help to tell stories. She sniffs them out.

I cannot get the ashtray clean. The barman stays black.

Here comes Dad's crock ...

He comes in at the door. His nails are black. His hair shines from oiliness.

"Dad? Hi, Dad."

Dad doesn't reply.

"Dad, I ..."

He just stares. He stares at the ashtray. He stares at the fan.

"Dad ..."

There's a furrow between his eyebrows. His eyes shine.

"Dad, your barman is black now ... Dad?"

His eyes well up. He frowns.

"Dad, your barman is black. I'm sorry, Dad."

He wipes his eyes and they look dry and empty again. He takes a deep breath, "Son ..."

The silence freezes around us. "Son, I lost my job."

Dad stands bent like a monkey. "I want to go and lie down a bit." He says nothing more.

Grade 12 – Hoërskool D F Malherbe, Walmer, PE

Though crime and poverty are still present in our country, South Africa has, since the release of Nelson Rolihlahla Mandela, become a Rainbow Nation. People are beginning to love and respect one another, irrespective of race or religion. Nelson Mandela has succeeded in becoming one of the most highly respected leaders of all time. Almost every single South African sees him as a sign of hope and a light for the future.

Jonathan Shahim
Grade 11 – St Stithians College, Randburg

Keith Kila – Guguletu Comprehensive

Child of the pavement
Emmerentia Erasmus

She could have been fourteen years old ... or eight. You never really know with them, unless you carefully look at the face. But if you do look carefully there are always two pleading eyes that fill your thoughts afterwards. Dirty-white eyes, murky around the large, dark pupils with a mistiness that makes them look even more secretive. It is as if the mistiness allows you to see only what they want you to see. And what you see is only the pleading for a few cents, that nauseates you, awakens your conscience and digs inside you.

I rested my eyes on the red jacket because it was the only colour in the grey weather. The frizzy, wild hair stuck out from under a blue beanie and hung stringily against the naked neck. She constantly rubbed her dust-pale, bewildered hands to get some fleeting warmth. She sat curled up in the corner. I don't know how I knew that it was a girl. Maybe there was something feminine in her bearing.

She sat motionless and I wondered what thoughts polluted her mind. Was she dreaming of a bottle of glue to survive the unbearable cold? Or ... was she longing for the nurturing and gentleness which her life lacked? How do children like her land on the street? Does she really have no refuge? Did she herself choose her future or was it fate that decided? My questions floated around the quiet figure. It was as if I were waiting for a reaction. But there was still only the cold and the wind and the grey weather. I had to stop myself from doing something that was not asked of me.

And then I saw the blue beanie move.

Her head turned slowly to the left, as if she had heard my thoughts. Her dull eyes turned towards me, but they were as expressionless as two marbles. Yet there was a softness around the corners of the mouth, almost a calmness. I wondered whether, hidden somewhere, there was not a trace of emotion.

I forgot my inhibitions, my background, my education and my lifestyle and counted my steps across the dirty bricks. I crouched next to the red jacket. We saw each other ...

Then the siren of a police van tore through the night, and the moment of truth, of person meeting person, had come and gone.

Grade 11 – *Rhenish Girls' High, Stellenbosch*

In this world full of sadness and wars, in this world which is a gift from our Heavenly Father to us, I find many things that disturb me so much that my heart feels like exploding with anger and compassion. The Lord has given us His Holy Son as a gift but the world spurns this gift.

Sello Frangis
Grade 12 – *Marallaneng Senior Sekondêre Skool, Ficksburg*

Undulukil' uSlovo – Slovo has departed
Jeffrey Brilliant Tyesi

We are not brave, we are full of tears, we people of Africa,
we are not heroes in our mourning of Slovo.

Slovo, you assisted us at the birth of an agreement;
you laid the eggs and sat on them until the chickens
were hatched.
You spurred us on towards a new South Africa.

It is he, people of Africa, who fed you,
it is he who insisted on nests for you
while you were hiding and protecting yourselves.
Let there be no more tears, be quiet now.

Hamba kwedini yamaBomvana!
Hamba kwedini kaSlovo!

(freely translated fragment)

Grade 12 – *Masimanyane Senior Secondary School, Bisho*

Hope is lost
Deshandra Dass

We live in an age of tolerance, where the dilemmas caused by previous generations are being resolved. Everything you read in the press or see on television advertises the "new" South Africa as a place where no grudges are borne and everyone has accepted that all the people of the Rainbow Nation are equal, with the same rights. There is no longer any division of people by race or culture, creed or colour. We all live in harmony in the reborn land that is South Africa ... Frankly, I think it's a load of codswallop.

I can't suddenly change the way I view a person of a different colour just because we are supposed to accept the views and beliefs of that person. How can we possibly hope to change decades of racial tension and social prejudice by pretending to change the way we feel toward each other? All my life I have been surrounded by my own kind. Enclosed in that cocoon, I never had to associate with "Whiteys" or "Blacks".

But suddenly, people of colour have a say. We are allowed into places previously reserved for Whites, we have democratic votes, we can go to mixed schools, we can walk around without concern for police harassment. Because Blacks now have gained more power and an equal say, the Whites hope to be forgiven for the atrocities of their ancestors. Many of us have indeed managed to forgive and actually look to the future with hope. I am not one of these. For me, a member of the Indian minority, nothing has changed.

My people arrived in this country as indentured labourers, as slaves. It took hard work and an endless struggle for them to break out of that mould. But still we have nothing to show for our efforts. Apartheid saw to it that Whites were allowed to vote and had rights which Blacks could only dream of. Discriminatory action ensured that Whites got jobs, that Whites lived comfortably while people of colour toiled in a fruitless existence. In these times Indian people were not white enough to gain any special rights or privileges. We were treated in the same way as Blacks.

In 1990, all that started changing – Nelson Mandela was released from prison. Our first democratic election took place in 1994. Blacks and Whites now had equal rights and the era of unity had begun.

Then, though no one acknowledged it, everyone knew it was happening: we were reverting back to the same old system. Only, this time in the opposite way. Black people are now given the jobs. Black people now have status. And once again, the Indian minority is left in the cold. This time we are not black enough. How can I be expected to live contentedly in a country where the colour of my skin is still a hindrance in spite of the promise of equality for all?

I respect the views of the people who look into the future with hope and pride. One has to admire their optimism. But I find it increasingly difficult to lose my cynical view on life in South Africa as I daily see bigoted practices which refute everything this country is supposed to represent. I long for the day when we can drop the charade and can truly say that everyone in South Africa is treated equally. Then I will be able to say that I am genuinely proud to be a South African.

But until that day comes, I will wallow in my cynicism, waiting.

Grade 11 – *Westerford High, Rondebosch, Cape*

When one mentions the words "New South Africa" to foreigners, they probably think that everybody gets on very well with everybody else, and that Black and White get along very well indeed. South Africa is currently being presented as a country which has undergone a complete change. But foreigners don't know what happens to some of us Blacks in this country. We are still being treated as before – we are still being called vulgar names such as "kaffir".

Nomthetho Ntshoko
Grade 11 – *Westerford High, Rondebosch, Cape*

Isabel Carstens – Frank Joubert Art Centre

The tin cup
Heidi Swart

It's a shit place, this. Both inside and outside. The grass is thick, the chrome number two hangs skew, the post-box is broken, the wall needs a paint job. Faded Novilon, cracks full of Polyfilla, broken tiles, broken plugs, the carpet's edges fraying, the bathroom light full of mosquitoes and gnats. Lion Lager, Coke, brandy and old Viennas in the fridge, that's all. Cockroaches. Dad lies in his room, rotting in his own sweat and breath. Yes, it's a shit place, this. But it hasn't always been like this.

I am five. "Southern Districts' Cue-Ball Champion 1972," Dad reads the letters on the silver cup to me. Again he tells me the story of him and Johnny Grey. Black ball wins. And with "a shot that has never been recorded in the books before", Dad brought the trophy home. "Yes, Boet. You must just have a bit of guts. Take the pressure, then you can make it anywhere."

I am nine. I have lost against Wimpie Viljoen. I didn't see the hole in the tar. One moment I felt the sweat on the handlebars and then suddenly I got a mouth full of gravel and dust. Something is broken and the front wheel of the bike is buckled. I go and fetch dad's Cue-Ball Cup from the top of the TV and I know, next time there'll be nothing left of Viljoen. I'd rather not tell Dad.

I am fourteen. My left eye is swollen. My ribs are sore. Momberg hit me real hard. Scum! Called Dad and me names! If De Wet and whoever the other one was, hadn't pulled us apart, it would have been another story. But Cue-Ball is there. I lightly touch the stained silver. And then I know everything will be okay. Dad laughs at my eye.

I am fifteen. I see how the number nine on Tommie Laubser's back is getting smaller. I look down at my togs. The teacher's hand is on my shoulder: "Don't worry. Next game. Next game." Only later, when I stroke the string of letters in the silver, do I believe him. I don't tell Dad.

I am seventeen. She stands at the bicycle rack. I know she's just a goose. Her brown hair is curly. The wind blows it into her eyes, her mouth. She pushes it behind her ear. Her nails are long. She folds her arms tightly around her breasts. She laughs about something that another girl has said. It's just a goose, but my legs are wobbly.

"Do you want to go to the drive-in tonight? I can get my dad's Cortina."

She swings her head in my direction. Her eyes widen. They are blue.

"I don't think my dad will say yes. My mom and the rest are watching Dallas tonight and I've got to get the kids to bed for them, etcetera."

Someone calls her. Stuff you, doll. Later I switch off Dallas and sit with my dad's silver cup in my hands. Oh well, that blond chick in standard eight is also quite nice. Dad is sleeping.

I am eighteen. I can go and joll with Dad now. As usual, the boys all stand around the fire. Dad is on his twelfth Lager. He talks so loudly he could wake up a stone. It's just smoke and beer and dirty jokes. I hear Johnny Grey's name. Dad asks me to fetch the trophy ...

And then someone says it. The bastard looks at the silver cup and just says it, just like that: "But you stole that bloody thing from Theron. Mind you, it was quite a good trick. To this day he doesn't know where the damn thing is."

This is a shit place. There's a Coke stain on the table cloth, the toilet doesn't flush properly, there are rings on the coffee table, lots of bulbs are blown.

And there is a stained tin cup, which once was gleaming silver, standing on the TV.

Grade 12 – *Rhenish Girls' High, Stellenbosch*

Prospective foreign tourists to Africa probably visualise the following: a savage land; a land of adventure and the big five; long stretches of endless hills and mountains, covered in lush vegetation; majestic sunsets spread across the sky ... And this *is* what Africa is about – to a certain extent. But I want to suggest another view, another "Welcome to Africa":

A weary mother sits on the arid ground, clutching her emaciated child. Tears trickle down her gaunt face because she knows that her child is starving and weak, and that there is no more food. This is a common sight in many parts of Africa, a continent torn apart by civil wars and endless droughts.

Bradley Thorpe
Grade 11 – *St Stithians, Randburg*

The professional Bushmen
Anya Subotzky

The parching heat swallows the truckload of sunburnt tourists. Dust consumes camera bags, sunglasses, smiles. In this landscape, close and arching, eyes and souls are lost in vastness. Lying in its innocence, the pseudo-Bushman village offers a pathetic welcome to expectant guests: an empty circle of huts cut to the angle of tourist cameras. In the dirt and heat and puddles of shade, the Bushmen slink in huddles. And hidden beyond a hillside, their real tin-shack homes squat amidst desert-rejected litter.

The pack of tourists approach with smiles of practised fascination as the professional Bushmen begin their work, uniformed in shivering nakedness. And hastily stashed beneath a rock, their everyday Western clothes sneer in pity.

I am sick at the unfolding of this human zoo and my own nauseating wonder. Slowly, my silent dreams of a golden people crash to reality.

The Bushmen enact their ancient roles while the tourists observe from behind the safe barrier of the camera lens, held out by each like a disfigured weapon.

Click! Click! Click!

"Stand a little to the left, won't you?"

Click!

"Yes, next to my wife so that I can see she is taller than you."

Click!

"We've just got to support the dears, Harry. Won't this tortoise shell make a *unique* Christmas decoration?"

"Please dance for me? Oh, won't you sing? Come on, sing! Sing! *Sing* …"

But the children remain silent, shy, still. Click! And beneath their smiles, the Bushmen use their own clicks to communicate – soft, low and ironic.

I am caught in this desperate cross-fire. No human contact is possible beyond the barrier of lenses. I am betrayed by my own helpless wonder, my shameful observation, my need to believe these lies.

Eventually, I slink to a corner of stale shade, and hide my own shameful camera. Soon, tripping light-winged through the heat, a flutter of children gather around me. Softly in the shadows, over and over like a wail or whisper, they begin to sing, "Boesmanland, vat my hand ... Boesmanland ... Boesmanland ..."

And as the day begins to die, and the ancient sun dips past the hillside, I slip into a dream. The children shoot their laughing arrows, then sweep into a half-forgotten dance. A fire echoes the lingering day, brushed like blood across the evening.

As I lose myself in wonder, impish eyes spy my camera. Try as I may, I cannot hide it; the professional smiles insist on their due.

Laughing, I dutifully take their photo.

And laughing, they scatter off into the darkness.

Grade 12 – Westerford High, Rondebosch, Cape

"You have to be the very best and you have to excel in all fields. Your future depends on that." This is what drives and subconsciously motivates most teenagers. Just the cleverest, the fastest and the most gifted is considered successful. Millions pursue this ideal and yet, only a few really can make it to the top. That makes me wonder: Are we perhaps on the wrong track?

Karien Lubbe
Grade 12 – Hoërskool Durbanville, Durbanville

Earth to mankind

Megan Jones

In the mists of nothing,
Before the swift pace of time,
I was conceived by the thoughts of God
And created by his touch.

Fires wrought rock on my surface
And cold seas devoured me.
Out of this fiery passion and ice
Formed a bitter-sweet life:
Man, my redeemer – and destroyer.

As he grew and changed,
I nurtured him with my soil.
But he usurped, forgot me,
No longer hears me,
Though I call to him still.

      Grade 11 – *Pietermaritzburg Girls' High, Scottsville, Pmb*

Karl Mostert – Frank Joubert Art Centre

Woodstock Cave
Philip Samuel

My mother comes into the room. I can hear from the way she walks that she has plans, bright and breezy plans, and that nobody will be spared. I groan into my pillow but she plucks open the curtains and pushes the windows as if they were bar doors. "Get up! Get up!" she says, in that tone of voice. "We're going to climb Devil's Peak this morning."

Nice. I protest a bit and grumble, and hear my sister furiously slamming the bathroom door and screaming: "Why does everybody have to go walking just because one bloody person has gone off her rocker!"

My youngest brother throws his lithe young body over a chair and the sofa and looks up to the heavens: "Help me, please, somebody help me, help me-e," imitating the wailing of an electric guitar.

My mother remains unperturbed. She packs the rucksack. She coos like a dove. She babbles us into the car. But when she starts singing some stupid girl-guide song, my dad stops the car. "You are going too far now."

He turns towards us: "Just one more moan from you guys and I drop you off in Blouberg and then I can go and sit at home while you use up your energy by walking home."

We climb Devil's Peak in deadly silence. The sea is a special blue. Everywhere there are birds and flowers, begging for a biology assignment.

Woodstock Cave. At the entrance of the cave we cool down under the waterfall.

"I wonder for how many centuries people have stood here and looked over the bay," says my father.

"Yes, probably since the time of the Khoisan."

Something stirs in my memory. A children's rhyme, a bushman tale.

I hear the sound
of the stars.
The stars say: Tsau!
They say: Tsau! Tsau!
That's the sound that stars
make in summer.
They say: Tsau!
Tsau! Tsau!

Hihiii!
I'm a shaman
a Khoikhoi herbman
I bring this world
And the world on the other side of the world
Together, so that both may become real.

On the wall of the cave I see the shaman's drawing of a man with hooves, dancing with an eland. From here he must have seen Jan van Riebeeck land.

The waterfall runs down my back. There is an iron around my leg and a festering wound underneath it. They put the iron on in Zanzibar. Here in the Cape I was sold to Jan Schepping, a farmer from the district of Stellenbosch. One Sunday afternoon he called me. He said it was about the horse that had been neglected. He put me over a wine barrel. He took the horse-brush with the iron teeth and with great dedication scratched every inch of skin off my back. His wife came to pour a bucketful of salt water over the purple, bloody mess that was my back and then led him away, soothingly.
I move my back deeper under the cool waterfall and look out over the bay ...

"Where do you get that from?" shouts my mother.
My little brother comes from the back of the cave with a half-metre high Rastafarian hat that sinks right over his eyes and dark glasses on his nose, shaking his imaginary dreadlocks:

"I shot the sheriff
but I didn't shoot no deputy ..."

"The Rastas are going to put a spell on you. Your head will become as floury as this apple," my sister says cheekily, throwing her half-eaten apple into the grass.
"Can't we take home some of the dagga that is drying at the back of the cave?" she asks, deliberately. My mother hastily begins packing away our things and my little brother raps:

"Black by birth
Proud by choice ..."

We make our way home. It is almost as if I can hear the insects for the first time – signals from their antennae. And smell the faint scent of the fynbos …

Grade 12 – *Jan van Riebeeck, Cape Town*

Checkmate
Lenelle Foster

The guard at the parking area looked up as the two men walked past him. One of them, the one with the new Armani suit and the black briefcase, nodded to him. He nodded back. They walked towards a bottle-green BMW. The one on the driver's side struggled a bit and mumbled that someone should check this lock.

Strange that they don't have one of those alarm things, the guard thought. But he took no further notice of the men and continued to read his newspaper.

When the two men drove out of the parking area the man on the passenger side laughed. "It's like stealing candy off a baby! That was an effing nice touch, that bit about the lock. That guy didn't smell a thing. Charlie, you are a genius!"

"I would be a helluva lot happier once we get this car to Mechanics," said Charlie. "I don't smaak this driving around in broad daylight. What if someone recognises us?"

"Ag man, your problem in life is that you worry much too much."

"And who kicked up such a fuss 'cause he forgot his lucky charm? Hannes, you're a hypocrite, that's what you are!"

Charlie braked hard as an old lady suddenly appeared in front of them. Hannes frowned. "I might be a hypocrite but you're a lousy driver, man. Do you want to get us charged for manslaughter as well?"

"Can I help it if this auntie comes and pushes herself in front of me? I'm mos not a magician that knows what people are going to do next."

"Okay, Charlie man, fine! I understand. Your nerves are shot. But think, we just have to get this one done and then we've got enough money to get out," Hannes consoled him. "After this we are free and the world is our oyster." He fumbled in his jacket pocket and took out a small plastic bag and a lighter. He took something from the little bag and showed it to Charlie.

"Here, this will make you feel better."

"Are you out of your mind? In broad daylight! Anyway, I can't while I'm driving. What if I crash this baby?"

Charlie looked at the traffic lights. "Does this stuff never go green? You could swear it was a plot!" he mumbled.

Hannes pulled up his shoulders. "I don't know about this plot but if you don't want to smoke then I'll do it."

"And then I also get high? I told you mos, not while I drive, man. Anyway, who do you think will buy a car that stinks of dagga? Put the stuff away now, just now PAGAD will catch you!"

Charlie tapped on the steering wheel with his fingers. "Finally!" he said when the lights turned green. They drove around the corner and got to the following traffic light just in time to see it turn red.

"PAGAD won't catch me," Hannes said somewhat stupidly. "PAGAD is looking for the higher-ups, like Staggie."

"Is that so? And why are they then called People Against Gangsterism and Drugs? They are after you and your buddies, my mate. All of you!"

A man with a sign saying "HUNGRY, JOBLESS – PLEASE HELP!" slowly moved along the line of cars that had formed behind the BMW. He kept looking at a car and the passengers inside, and if he didn't notice any reaction, he moved further along the line. Finally he got to the BMW. He looked into the window. With his left hand he fumbled in the pocket of his pants. Suddenly he pulled open the door with his right hand and pressed a revolver against Charlie's head.

"Come on!" he said. "This is a hijacking, not a tea party! Get out the car, you yuppie scum!"

Grade 11 – *Rhenish Girls' High, Stellenbosch*

Mara

Anica Bester

It was a Kalahari sunset, with tufts of blond grass and a blue sky, turning orange. Birds sang their last song and the cicadas softened their shrilling. A light gust of wind almost imperceptibly stirred the branches of the thorn trees.

A donkey cart moved along the red Griekwastad dirt road, passing the prickly-pear orchards and the stone dam. And that is where, in a box under the thorn tree at the gate of the cattle pen, Anna Bosman and her husband found her. Anna picked her up and wrapped her in an old patchwork blanket. "Siembamba, mamma se kindjie," Anna sang softly as the sky turned grey all around them and the donkey cart shuddered along the path home to the farm.

By the time they reached Rusoord with the little bundle, the crickets were screaming and one could no longer see further than the pepper tree near the cart-shed. They knocked on the wooden panels of the screen door and left her in the care of the white people.

There on the farm, she grew up amongst the other children – who did not accept her. Liesbet and Dirk were older than she was, and Susan was the youngest. And then there was Johannes, the oldest. Johannes, with the big hands and the blue eyes and the full, blunt face. Johannes, who once brought back a hare from the veld for her.

They called her Mara. She never spoke, but you could see the rays of the sun playing in her midnight eyes. She was not like the others. Her mouth was too large, her eyes too dark and her hair curled too wildly. Everybody knew that she belonged to another world and nobody tried to understand her. That is why, during the day, she played with the brown children: Sanna, Miriam, Mietjie and Stuurman. They made little wreaths of thorn-tree flowers at the zink dam, where the finches screeched in the reeds and the women came to scrape sheep's heads.

She was scared when thunderstorms threatened. And when it thundered she would creep under the bed in the guest-room. But later, when it started to rain, she would run around and play the flute that Stuurman had made for her.

At night, when they had eaten and the others sat around the kitchen table, talking by the light of the oil lamp, she would sit on the veranda

Talitha Kotzé – Frank Joubert Art Centre

with her arms around her knees. She would peer into the night and listen as if it were the first time that she had seen or heard the darkness.

Some afternoons she sat in the vegetable garden where Gert Springbok was working. He would tell her about the worlds that lay beyond the Kalahari horizon. Although she sat staring out in front of her, making patterns in the sand with her toes, he knew she was listening carefully.

It was in her seventeenth year on the farm when Johannes said to her one evening: "The moon is full tonight, Mara. Come, I will show you how it rises there at the dry river bed."

"Yes, Maratjie, go," said her adoptive father. "You never seem to get enough of staring at the moon."

But his wife looked on silently as they walked off.

They sat waiting in the silence on a large rock near the river which flowed only once every seventeen years. And then it rose. At first they could only see its bald pate and then, later, it hung above the horizon, full and blunt, like Johannes's face.

"Come and lie here next to me on the sand," Johannes whispered. And he began undoing the little pearl buttons on the dress that had belonged to Liesbet. "You won't tell anybody, hey Maratjie?" His laughter cut through the silence.

She smelled the moist tufts of grass. She clung to the stars that hung low over the thorn trees. She heard a cow lowing for its calf and an owl calling restlessly. The umbrella-thorn cast its shadows in the light of the moon …

At dusk of the first full moon after she felt the life in her belly, the clouds gathered and water poured over the dry veld. Mara ran through the downpour towards the windpump at the cattle pen. She climbed the gleaming steel stairs. On the edge of the platform she stopped and looked up at the full moon.

"Siembamba, mamma se kindjie …" Or was it just the wind singing? She spread her arms, gently rocking herself and then she lay into the wind. The night held her tightly, comfortingly enfolding her, taking her to another world, beyond the farthest horizon.

Grade 11 – *Hoër Meisieskool La Rochelle, Paarl*

Think before you leap
André Kritzinger

The lift moved up, up, slowly. Much too slowly for his liking. Or maybe not. He didn't know anything about anything any more. These days he felt so insecure! If he could just get the results as quickly as possible, then the nerve-racking wait would be over. But what if the results were positive ... No, he should rather delay it for another week or two. Maybe he would be able to prepare himself better. Living with it was not his biggest problem, what worried him was what the others at home would say.

"Excuse me," he brushed against a large black woman in front of him and for a moment he saw Angeline's face looking at him with its big brown eyes. At the same time a whirl of mixed emotions welled up in him. His passionate love for Angeline, but also the fear and uncertainty about the future. He walked along the long passage. Right, left. At last he got to the glass door and saw that there were already five people sitting in the waiting room. With his hand on the shiny knob, he went inside before his courage could leave him.

He quickly picked up a magazine and paged through it blindly. "Smoking is bad for you. Smoking causes cancer." He wished it was such an illness, something that everybody understood or at least accepted. An illness that did not evoke so many questions. He looked at the others in the waiting room. Their expressions differed; only the nervous paging through tattered magazines seemed to bind them together.

Thoughts went through his head: "How could you do this to us? What overcame you? I thought I had brought you up better. Who was it? Why? When?" He became anxious and fearful. He had to get out! Breathe in deeply ... breathe out. He looked around quickly to see whether anybody had noticed his fear, but everybody seemed to be preoccupied with his or her own problems. Maybe *this* is the problem with the country. Many problems could be prevented if people would just care more for each other and think less about themselves. At least his problem could have been prevented.

It was supposed to have been a wonderful, romantic evening. Just he and Angeline. A candlelight dinner. If it had only stayed like that. Why had he not stopped? He had known that things were going too far but he had not stopped the dangerous process. If only she had *told* him that she had AIDS. But he realised again that that was no excuse. "Look before you leap." How often had he not read or heard those words!

"Mr Reynolds, you can come in now." The words hit him in the face like cold water. The moment of reckoning had arrived. He closed the door behind him.

"Good afternoon. I shall be brief. I have your test results here and it seems as if there is good news and bad news."

He had known all along, he had the HIV virus. The good news was probably that he did not have full-blown AIDS yet. But he knew, it was just a matter of time, then everything would be over.

"Mr Reynolds, the good news is … your HIV test is negative."

Negative! Negative? That is wonderful. How was that possible? He did not give a damn. He would live! He had got a second chance.

"The bad news, however, is … Angeline is pregnant."

Grade 11 – *Hoërskool De Kuilen, Kuilsriver*

Being a teenager is not easy. "The future is in your hands!" We, the youth of South Africa, have been told this so many times that the words have lost their impact. Just another cliché. Still, this generation's children are the next generation's adults. We'll then be responsible for this new nation, a nation that has emerged like a phoenix from the remains of the old one – which scarred past generations with its injustice, corruption and violence. Our new nation is not perfect either. Violence still occurs – random, senseless violence, taxi wars and gang fights. But this nation is headed in the right direction, our new leaders have learnt from the mistakes of the past government and are doing their best.

Cameron Gilbert
Grade 11 – *Westerford High, Rondebosch, Cape*

Nadia Price – Battswood Art Centre

You have so much more
Nili Dahan

You sip your cappuccino with great sophistication. Your fifth finger protrudes delicately from the rest, and moves up and down with each sip, conducting our flimsy conversation. We dissolve into the languid atmosphere of the dimly-lit coffee shop, as your words twirl effortlessly from your cup.

To capture this moment is as impossible as trying to trap the warmth that lingers around an empty mug. Your urgent eyes dart around the room, snatching information from each table. Who's here? Whom are they with?

I watch you becoming totally distracted, as I sink back in the cushioned chair – a disappointed mother.

Everything that your father has attempted to teach you over the years is now neatly concealed behind the perfect foundation make-up on your face. But your hands fidgeting with the ashtray on the table look like your father's. Not even your favourite red varnish can hide this.

I contemplate the car ride on the way here. How I had caught a glimpse of your father's smiling eyes in the rear-view mirror. Gesturing to an empty playground, he told us how he had taken you there when you were small. I recall that yellowing photo of the two of you in the park, with your cheek pressed against his, your tiny mouth pulled into a grin, aching with happiness.

In the car you rudely demonstrated your impatience as you threw your head back and swung your body forward in order to reach the volume knob of the radio. Callously, you raised the volume with one defiant twist. The blast of noise slapped me into reality; your father's coarse hands jerked the steering wheel slightly and then adjusted their grip. You stared composedly ahead, whilst bathing your hands in floral-scented hand cream.

When we climbed out of the car, you shook your frustrated head vigorously, like a wet dog shakes itself dry. Then your crinkled forehead ironed out as your father's battered car clattered away.

When a clan of girls from school approached our table, you jumped up in genuine falseness. High-pitched greetings pierced the air and exaggerated Hollywood air-kisses were exchanged. My vague how-are-you's were brushed aside by their predictable sing-song answers. Your father and the car ride seemed as distant as a disturbing dream.

You stared after them in admiration as they scurried off to another table to repeat their rehearsed enthusiasm and I remember how your eyes, the colour of dark coffee, brimmed with frivolous fun … I stared at you vacantly, thinking of how much you were missing out on. But you will never know.

You have always been a stubborn pupil whenever your father, the teacher, presented his lecture. He could never control this single-pupil class. The telephone screech usually signified the end of the period and you would run to your room and slam the door behind you.

You are still staring longingly at the girls, turning the back of your coiffed head to me and I want to cry out, "Don't you understand? You have so much more than they!"

But these words are suffocated before they leave my throat. Instead, pointless chatter flutters between us and our words are as cool and glossy as the pages of a fashion magazine.

Your father – and the wisdom of his age – wait patiently for us in the car.

Grade 12 – *King David High, Linden, Jhb*

I, a living arrow
Jodi Rosenberg

I sit, staring at my ashen reflection in the dressing-table mirror. My door, slammed shut in her face, is locked to ensure that I am left totally alone. The replay of words and ugly comments pierces my throbbing brain and makes my swollen eyes bulge and strain.

I cannot understand why I feel so abandoned when I myself have chosen to be locked in confinement.

I try to ignore the persistent knocking at the door. Each thump irritates me, drives my heart further into my throat, chokes me, making my tears burn.

The silence from my room shuns the gentle voice that wants to console me, even after all the things that I should not have said.

I am furious with the hateful person looking at me from my mirror. I remember the obnoxious comments and hurtful words that polluted my mouth and mind while we assaulted each other. Did she mean those serrated insults that shredded me to pieces, or were they just a sharp defence against my blatant blasts? I hope she realises that I did not mean all those insults that I voiced so convincingly.

Why do most of the things that we attempt to do together, drive us further apart?

She is the bow from which I, a living arrow, am sent forth. She is the light in which I have bloomed. My world would be barren and dry without her tender nurturing.

We are both unique and diverse. I wish we could learn to accept our differences, avoid the thunderous skies, and find the rainbow in each other's heart.

Grade 12 – King David High, Linden, Jhb

Pink-Roses Panado

Cecile de Vries

Suddenly the dusty photograph in the little frame turns into something more than just a picture. Few things cut life open like a photograph. It is almost as if Ouma were here in her often repaired wheelchair, wearing her pink-roses gown and her thin smile. Just like four years ago when she left us.

The memory is still crystal clear. It was the year when we, her swarm of grandchildren, were so furious because she had made the same present for all of us ... bed-socks! A pair of crocheted bed-socks! Mine had a posy of pink roses embroidered on them. Ouma got the pattern from Mrs van Jaarsveld, the *dominee's* wife.

Everybody on the flat Free State plains wore those things. No wonder! Your only protection against those cruel winters and the swells of dejection were bed-socks, one of few things that could comfort those who suffered from corns ... Indeed, they were the rural equivalent of Panado.

But a year or two ago, thin mannequin bodies and the latest dance steps became important to me. At the end of an evening, hours after our black school shoes had been exchanged for black high-heels, our toes would be all scrunched up and numb. Mother, who always thought she knew everything, once more recommended bed-socks for this ailment. "Don't be a sleepyhead and be caught out without bed-socks," the saying went.

Then the cold overtook me too and forced me to abandon my shiver-blue bitterness about the present, and I put on the crocheted Parys-socks. I have to admit that, at first, I only wore them secretly ... why would a model in the making wear baby booties!

My mother always said, "If your feet are warm, then the rest of your body is also warm." Even your heart seems warmer. Because, if your toes start thawing one by one in your cuddle-socks, you suddenly have more than enough ideas for the five-page essay on "Life in the new South Africa". (I know that I can definitely free myself in the new South Africa when I wear my dream-socks.)

I wonder what Ouma would say about the bed-socks they make today? For example, in Germany they come with rubber soles, screaming in the latest fashionable colours. With those on your feet, you don't feel the puddle which Rover left behind on the kitchen floor. Of course the jewel of all bed-socks remains the fine, crocheted type ... like Ouma's. Embroidered with a posy of pink roses?

Today I am happy that Ouma introduced me to the Parys-Panado. Little did she know, she with her crippled hands, that such a little present would one day mean so much to me. Of course I now curse myself. Why did I never thank her? Perhaps with a posy of pink roses ...?

Grade 11 – *Crawford College, Pretoria*

Sindile Ngamlana – Guguletu Comprehensive

To my mind, joblessness is similar to the pain of losing a parent. If pupils leave school while they are still in the lower grades, they are not able to find a job, and spend their time roaming around in the townships. They get involved in crime and are soon known as "tsotsis" or "imigavela".

I blame the parents for not disciplining their children. Some parents spoil their children. I don't mean that they should always be cross or punish their children, but they should realise that parents are the ones who determine how their children will turn out. I also call on teachers to introduce their pupils to the business world and to the courses offered by technikons and universities. This might encourage them to study – something which is of great importance for their futures, because everything about an uneducated person is sour.

Mziwamadoda Mene
Grade 12 – *Ikamvalethu Finishing School, Thornton*

A six-year-old does not know
Debbie Berman

Like hawks they smelt the fresh, young, innocent blood of my brain, and attacked ... I was too young to understand why my mother's friends were pouring soap all over my brain, or why they were scrubbing vigorously to remove the non-existent stains. All I knew was that they were comforting a pain that I did not feel, and quelling a fear that did not exist. They, through their eagerness to help (it's always fun to be in on the scandal), caused only confusion.

A six-year-old does not know what the word "alcoholic" means. A six-year-old does not care if her father greets imaginary people loudly on the street. A six-year-old does not understand why the Nice-Man-Whom-She-Must-Tell-All-Her-Problems, is suddenly issuing a court order that forbids her from going to see her father.

Looking back at these events now, I can understand why I was suddenly surrounded by strange faces all wanting to "help" me.

I loved visiting my father every second week. He always had loads of empty bottles that he kept just for me, and I would fill these with water and tiny pieces of paper that I had coloured in. I would play with the strange-smelling bottles, watching the little pieces of paper floating softly up and down the glass. I always did this while my father went to talk to the Stupid-Manager-Who-Said-That-He-Hadn't-Paid-When-He-Had.

Every second week it was so exciting to find out which hotel Daddy now stayed in, and – of course – to meet the new Stupid-Manager.

Yet, as things will always change, they did. It was only three years later that I finally realised why all my mother's friends had been comforting me. But by then it did not really matter, as I hadn't seen HIM for three years.

That, of course, was not the last I saw of him. Like a crocodile lurking under the water he occasionally emerged for some air. And then he would take a great gulp of oxygen with assorted molecules – such as our emotions, our hope and trust. Then, with the promise to return, the crocodile would submerge. Of course, the crocodile always kept his word – but in his own way. Sometimes he would emerge a week, sometimes a couple of months, later. Once he emerged after four years – just in time to prevent me from totally forgetting him.

I have lost count of the number of years he has now been submerged.

Yet I cannot help wondering if I will ever see him again. Would I turn around and walk away as I – in dark hours – have pictured myself doing? Or would I be uncontrollably drawn to him, voluntarily opening the doors and be vulnerable yet again?

Grade 12 – King David High, Linden, Jhb

It is the duty of the parents to give their children a good foundation. One can say that parents who do not show their children the right way, are giving them diluted milk or sour milk. Such parents might be under the impression that they are giving their children creamy milk because they are so kind. But they are actually spoiling the children's future.

Welcome Meme
Grade 12 – Ikamvalethu Finishing School, Thornton

The beginning
Marcelle Olivier

When the writer starts writing she does not have anything specific in mind. There is no guidance, no smoothly tarred road that takes her on flights of fantasy, no facts and no words. Nothing is stored in her thoughts with which she can work; there is just an empty, unhelpful computer screen that irritates her endlessly with its flickering orange square.

The writer stares outside, past her table, in search of an idea for her story. She pushes aside the netting in front of the window and looks at her neglected garden. Maybe there are stories hidden there, between the dense creepers against the wooden fence or even in the bit of loquat tree she can see from here. Maybe the lawn also has a story, she thinks. But the grass has died in the heat and the devil-thorns decorate its surface.

Later, the writer gives up looking for the story in the garden. She looks farther, over the fence, at the farm. Where the farm once was visible over the brown fence, it is almost completely hidden behind crooked trees and dense bushes and white stones now. The writer is disappointed. She has never even noticed that the farm had vanished. Oh, she knows that the sweet vineyard is still there, but if she cannot see it from where she sits, then there is no story.

The enmeshed branches and leaves that block her view interest her. The shades of green and brown, the black shadows and patterns of the seed pods and the bird shapes awaken an image. It's an image of yellow-green leaves and pink Matisse clouds and dark, steaming summer rain and …

As suddenly as the painting has tinted her memory, it vanishes. The screen flickers its monotonous pattern and the writer's fingers lie stupidly and emotionlessly in front of her. "Edit document or press Esc to use menu - Edit document or press Esc to use menu" she reads at the bottom of the screen. There is nothing to edit, nothing on the screen or in her head.

After the writer has read the newsletter lying next to her, the phone rings. It is her friend's little brother. The writer knows that the little brother likes her and tries her best to amuse him. After a while she talks to her friend. The friend tells her that she is doing her annual spring cleaning. The writer has an idea for a story but continues talking. They arrange to meet at the village waterfall, and then they begin gossiping about their men-friends.

It is good to talk to someone, she thinks.

After the conversation she goes back to her computer, but she has already forgotten the idea. It has cancelled itself. But the writer feels better about herself and that is why she can start writing about herself. She feels good because people still phone her and it is not always she who has to feed her friendships.

Suddenly the grass outside no longer looks so dry and she can distinguish pieces of vineyard in the jigsaw puzzle on the other side of the fence. A little yellow bird has come to sit on the lawn and is hopping about in the shadows of the trees. The fingers of the writer move almost automatically over the keys in front of her.

She starts writing about herself and tells a story about a writer who did not know what to write about: When the writer starts writing she does not have anything specific in mind. There is no guidance, no smoothly tarred road that takes her on flights of fantasy, no facts and no words. Nothing is stored in her thoughts with which she can work; there is just an empty, unhelpful computer screen that irritates her endlessly with its flickering orange square …

Grade 12 – *Rhenish Girls' High, Stellenbosch*

Christopher Wadely – Frank Joubert Art Centre

Do you also see the red flower?

Nicolette Maartens

"Look, Lizzie! Today the trees are green and the flowers are opening up. Look, the children are rolling on the grass. They are running and teasing each other. Listen to the soft sounds of joy. Birds are singing in the trees. People are laughing at jokes. Listen, there is a cricket playing on its violin, a cicada … and a butterfly flying by, soundlessly.

"Lizzie, I so much want you to smell the fresh air around us, the crushed grass, and feel the rough stem of the huge, old cypress. I scratch the bark. It smells of … blood? Here amongst the white gravel grows a red flower, Lizzie. I pick it for you. Hold it against your cheek so that you can feel the satin of its leaves and own its smell."

The girl with the thin hands got up. It looked as if she wanted to embrace the sun that stroked her cold arms. "Can you feel how deliciously warm the sun is shining, Lizzie? This summer we will get a nice, brown tan, hey?"

She stretched out her arms and ecstatically spun around in a fragile circle. She sank to her knees, sighing. Her large, confused eyes were full of fear, her fingers were desperately holding on to her slight body. Slowly she rocked to and fro. "Why don't we sing, Lizzie?

"Tula tu, tula mtwana,
tula tu, dadewethu,
u baba usebuya tula msana
tula tu, tula …

"Is it not the right one?

"Sleep little baby, don't say a word
Momma's gonna buy you a mockingbird
and if that mockingbird won't sing …
"Okay, then we'll sing something else.

"Siembamba, mamma se kindjie
Siembamba, mamma se kindjie
draai sy nek om, gooi hom in die sloot,
trap op sy kop, dan is hy dood …

"Do you remember, Lizzie? Mommy always used to sing that for us when we were small." She pressed her hands over her ears. "But Mom doesn't sing any more, never.

"Our first day at school … The teacher put an L on your forehead and a B on mine. Do you remember how it became a game later and we swapped the letters? And when we played hide-and-seek and one of us got caught, do you remember how they had to guess which one of us it was?

"In Grade 7 you cut your hair, and I cried for a long time. Mom asked why I was crying. She did not understand. That night I asked you whether you no longer wanted to be like me. You came with the scissors that evening. Dad scolded us later, and then we cried and you said that you did not want to be different from me. Me and you, … and me."

Black clouds moved in front of the sun.

"But Lizzie, you promised! We promised … always to love each other. Never, ever to separate! Why did you go away? Why did you break what was perfect?"

She looked up. Slowly she read the words aloud: "Here lies Elisabet Brink. Beloved daughter and twin sister of Betsie. Rest in peace, Lizzie."

The blade flashed. She was dizzy. Thoughts, colours, forms lapped against the beach of her thoughts.

They found her on the grave of her twin sister, a pathetic bundle, with gravel in one hand and a knife in the other. There were trickles of blood on the gravel, like fingers reaching out, and red petals, blown about, forgotten.

Grade 11 – *Hoërskool Voortrekker, Dorpspruit*

Peace

No war in peace
No death in peace
No tears in peace
No suicide in peace
Peace – the solution

That's the way to freedom
The road to liberation:
No gun or explosive
Common sense plays its role
Peace for the People

Peace in Africa
Peace to the People
Peace and freedom
Peace and unity
Peace and power
Sing it to the world!
(*a fragment*)

> Jeffrey Brilliant Tyesi
> Grade 12 – *Masimanyane Senior Secondary School, Bisho*

The passage of life
John Vorster

Panic-stricken, he grabs his chest. He falls so hard that the dust rises from the carpet in the passage. Anxiously his eyes look for a way out but the only light is from the sickle of the moon playing like a scythe on his chest. He tries to lift his hands one more time. But the time to raise his hands has passed. When the dust starts settling there is a sudden beating of the heart again. When it stops, he smiles and breathes his last breath.

He walks down the passage again and stares at the wallpaper which looks as if it has been stuck there for a life-time. He sees the toys that lie forgotten in the passage and thinks about the days when he himself was a child. Days of growing up with a load of responsibility because of the great things expected of him. And as he walks on, the dusky passage reminds him of the long days when he persuaded himself that his life would meet his expectations.

He was a man of integrity. Somebody to reckon with. After all, he had done everything, convinced that these were his dreams coming true. But like the potplant in the passage next to Room 36, yearning for something, he had pushed himself too far, until he was just a barren still life, a mediocre work of art in a gallery with only still lives.

Society finally took its toll: He never even realised that he was looking for happiness in the wrong places. And then, one day he stood at a fishpond and looked at the fish, swimming about. That's when he saw her, so full of life. Her eyes were as lively as torches. Yes, he wanted to remember them as torches. Not only do torches shine but they also dance as if entering eternity.

That day his passions were awakened. Just for one moment he wished to be part of her passion, her love for that which had long died within him.

His heart aches with longing, as if it had happened only yesterday. He sees himself, this time from a distance, pinned to a place by his own stupefied mind – the place where he had stood loyally for so many years. He feels the uncertainties and habits of many years engage in a heavy battle with the free will which everybody has but which some discover only too late.

How long had they stood opposite each other that day and not said a word? He had only managed a smile in reply to hers, and that only after she had turned to walk away.

More years had passed – years in which he had committed himself with new dedication to his life's task. Needless to say he had never felt such freedom again. And the downward path of his life had started even before the peak was visible. But no downhill is completely downhill. Some have knolls and hills *and* opportunities to return to a high point.

And that is what happens when he feels the pain in his heart. It is a pain which pulls him down violently there in the passage. It feels as if his soul is torn in two as he fights against the weakness overcoming him. He desperately struggles for the passage door. He had been told in his youth that it was never too late – and this thought flashes through his desperation: Maybe, even just for a moment, he could be part of something he desperately needs. Again hope leaps up in him, the hope that he can still grab at the one big chance in his life, long after the initial offer.

As he blinks his eyelids for the last time he feels his life draining from him. But sometimes, in the last moment of need, there *is* a way out. A door opens unexpectedly into the passage and a woman's face becomes visible in the dull light. As she approaches, the passage seems to be illuminated by a torch.

That is the image that greets him as his eyes flicker for the last time. The sudden knowledge that he has found what his being has been seeking, moves him so strongly, that once more his heart triumphantly pumps blood through his veins.

Grade 12 – *Hoërskool Jan van Riebeek, Cape Town*

Front: "Stop"

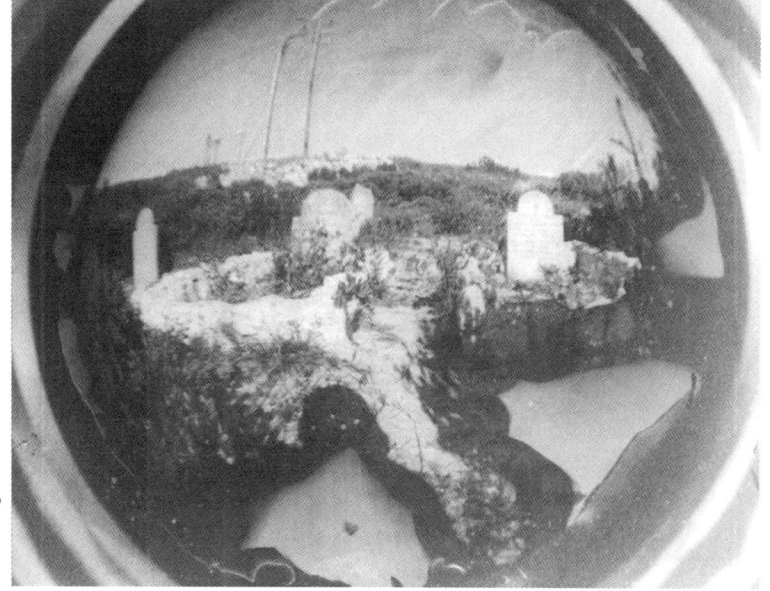

Back: "Stop"

Brendon Bentley – Frank Joubert Art Centre

The meal
Pieter Vermaak

There is an autocophagus in my cupboard. I see he has already been eaten half-way. I close the cupboard.

"Open the cupboard!" he says. I hesitate but realise that the autocophagus won't do me any harm.

"Thank you very much," he says sincerely, as the door swings open.

"No problem."

I go to the kitchen to make coffee. But the autocophagus prefers rooibos tea because coffee keeps him awake at night. He interrupts his meal to drink the tea. He likes the tea and asks for more. I make more tea. Only after he has drunk the third cup do I realise that I am late for school.

The autocophagus in my cupboard apologises. I tell him it's not his fault, but I actually know that it is and silently curse him.

Nobody at school is particularly excited about the idea that there is an autocophagus in my cupboard. I think most of them don't even know what it is. One guy says: "What's so special about that? My cousin also has one."

And I know immediately that it's a flagrant lie.

At home I go to visit the autocophagus before I take off my jacket. He has been eaten more than three-quarters and is apparently still very hungry. He shows signs of loneliness and I feel a little sorry for him but I do not forget that he is responsible for my detention on Friday. We chat for a long time about all kinds of things. The autocophagus is an entertaining talker.

I eat my lunch quickly so that we can continue the conversation, but the autocophagus teaches me to speak while I eat. He himself is very good at that. He says that he had a tragic childhood; his parents left him when he was only three years old. It is a moving tale.

"Do you see yourself as a cannibal?" I ask the autocophagus. He ignores the question and asks whether I could make him some coffee.

"But you said that coffee keeps you awake at night," I say.

"Yes, but tonight I want to stay awake."

"Why?" I try not to sound too curious.

"Keep your nose out of other people's business!" he answers indignantly. The rest of the day I leave him alone.

Night comes but I cannot sleep. I am scared.

In the morning I am very tired. But I laugh at my cowardice during the night and open the cupboard to greet the autocophagus. The cupboard is empty. Of course he stayed awake the whole night to finish his meal, I think. I am sad. The autocophagus was like a friend to me.

I climb into the cupboard and close the doors. It is very dark. I try to feel what the autocophagus felt. There is really not much you can do in a cupboard. I fidget.

Much later I realise it's Friday and that I should have gone to school. I also realise that I am going to miss detention.

I feel at home in the cupboard. I start chewing my nails although I haven't done that for a long time. I chew them slowly, to the quick ...

Grade 12 – *Hoërskool De Kuilen, Kuilsriver*

The Romany Creams
Petro Faasen

Cólette looks around her in the small hours of the night. She cannot see anything but she knows exactly what the room looks like, which posters are up, what chocolate papers are stuck where, which dried roses hang where and why they hang there. She also knows exactly who lies where. Thinking about the positions they lie in gives her a sense of satisfaction. Late at night is when she, Fat Let with the pimple-plague, gets her chance to laugh at them.

Her marshmallow hand reaches for the little cupboard next to her bed. She opens the drawer and carefully fumbles for her torch. She swears softly as she bumps her hand against the top of the drawer, scared that she will wake them. Before you know it they will want to share her cookies!

Her stomach growls. She is dying of hunger. The kitchen matron thought it was a good idea to put her on a diet. She even called her in to "talk to you in private, you poor dear". Cólette just agreed with everything. Now all she gets are boiled vegetables and brown bread without jam. And she does not even get a glass of milk, because "water is better for the skin". And when the other girls get toffee pudding or chocolate pudding or ice cream, she gets a pear or an apple or an orange, and a little knife. Always a little knife with a yellow handle. The other girls get custard with their pudding, and a spoon.

With the help of the torch Cólette easily finds the Romany Creams which she had bought that afternoon on her "daily walk" while the others were practising hockey. She tears open the packet. Her fat fingers vanish between the cookies like hungry worms in a bowl of greens. She puts a whole cookie in her mouth. Her teeth crunch on it. After chewing hastily, she swallows hard. The half-chewed crumbs scratch her throat.

Cólette does not like to share a room, neither with one girl nor with many girls. She always feels that they think they are better than she is. When she comes into the room they immediately stop what they are doing. Sometimes she hears them laughing just before she comes into the room. She knows that they are laughing about her. "Stupid Fat Let with the pimple plague!"

Mostly, she is happy that she is not part of such a clique, but sometimes she wishes that she were. At least they wouldn't laugh at her all the time.

But this is during the day; at night things are much better. Much better. Then, it is her turn. She can become Cólette, the girl with the pretty, modern name. Just like Surané and Anandé and Marílette. She has seen to it that her name also has one of those little accents and ends with an -ette. In the night she is no longer plain Let. Maybe they will like her more like this and will give Anna, who has her granny's name, a kick in the pants and tell her: "Sorry, but we like Cólette better."

Cólette. It is as if this name and the darkness make her stronger. She wants to laugh again. The suppressed noises make her sound like a vampire, she thinks. If she were one she could have sucked out their blood and left them lying there, lifeless. The matron would probably die a million deaths about the "poor dears, who were untimeously plucked from the garden of our sweet Lord Jesus". And every new moon another one would go. Then everybody would be dead except Cólette.

She sighs. The other children would say it was because she was so fat – the vampire simply couldn't get to her veins …

She pops another cookie into her mouth. "F… them."

Yet another cookie vanishes into her mouth. She lets the torch shine onto Surané. It's at her that she laughs most at night: Queen of the bees. The light shines on Surané's face. Cólette's face distorts with pleasure. A string of spit stretches from Surané's open mouth to her pillow. By the light of the torch it looks like a thread of gold to Cólette. Just think, "Did you hear what Surané does while she sleeps?" And then she would tell them.

She sighs again. Who would believe her anyway?

Soon she is bored with Surané and the golden thread and she shines the torch onto Marílette. But first her hand vanishes into the Romany Creams again. She presses three cookies into her cheeks. She struggles to chew.

Cólette begins at the bottom, shining her torch on Marílette's feet. Slowly she moves the beam. But as she gets to Marílette's face, she turns around and dives under the blankets without switching off the torch. Something has got stuck in her wind-pipe. Too scared to make a noise - what if they found out and told the matron?! - she stifles her coughing, which turns into a rattle.

And that is how they found her the next morning, under the blanket, the light of the torch reduced to a glimmer, the Romany Creams cradled like a baby in her cold arms.

Grade 12 – *Hoërskool De Kuilen, Kuilsriver*

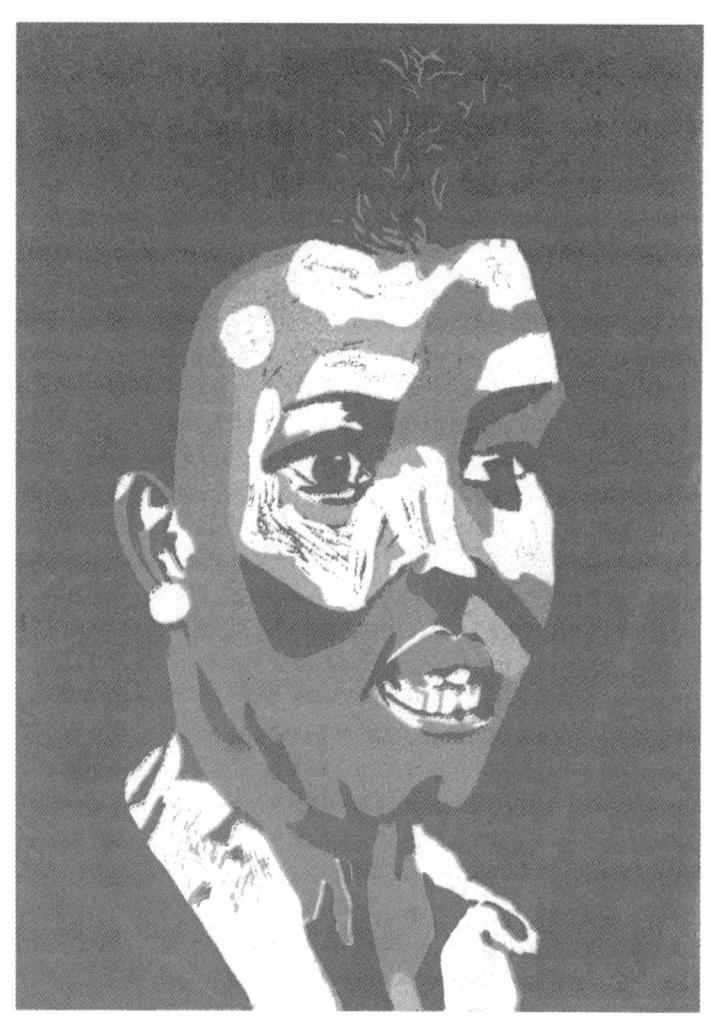

Natalie Nicholas – Battswood Art Centre

A banquet for two
Ansulie du Preez

One day, long, long ago, in the middle of the thick forest, there lived - amongst many others – a potter (female) and a movie critic (male). Their skins were as white as snow, their hair as black as tar, and their lips as red as blood. They both lived on the green pine-tree side of the forest in new-old houses, decorated in shades of brick-red, ocean-blue and off-white. They had roman blinds hanging in front of their windows.

Every Thursday, the movie critic would visit his father after he had removed his ear-, nose-, toe- and back-rings. And every Thursday night he ate at the house of the potter. However, Thursday happened to be the day on which the potter put on her avocado-and-mud face mask, which caused seeing-blindness in her for a day and a night. The potter always prepared delicious vegetarian meals and served them on the dinner service she herself had made from ozone-friendly clay. The movie critic always brought her a magical blackberry flower that aggravated her condition of seeing-blindness.

One day, while the potter was busy with a new creation (due to the fact that it is still incomplete, no further details may be made public about it) a forest angel appeared to her. On the insistence of this angel the potter walked to the house of the movie critic. She looked through the keyhole of the front door and saw that a fashion designer and the movie critic lived together.

She stumbled back home. Her heart turned into a heavy block of ice and her eyes were so dry that she had to put in some eye drops. She sank onto the black chair in front of the TV set. And when she came to, it was already dusk. She got up and walked to the phone to call her best friend with whom she could share her secrets and who was always prepared to listen. But her phone was cut off because she had forgotten to pay the account. This was on Tuesday.

On Thursday she did not put on her face mask so that her eyes would not deceive her. By lunch time she was prepared. The poisonous brew was in the fridge. She had prepared a delicious vegetarian dish, too, that was ready to be served on the dinner service she had made herself from ozone-friendly clay. When the movie critic appeared with the blackberry flower that he always brought for her, she took it to the kitchen. There she pressed the flower into liquid nitrogen and then she let it drop on the tiled floor and watched it shatter into a thousand pieces. She found it utterly satisfying not to be deceived by her own eyes.

But later that night when, as was usual, the movie critic asked her to put back his rings, she started to cry. The movie critic did not notice this. She picked up the back-ring, held it for a while against her lips and then dipped one point of the ring into the poison. Her hands were wet from the tears which had dripped onto them. She was on the point of putting back the ring, when her hand slipped and she pricked herself.

The potter died immediately.

The movie critic and the fashion designer lived together happily ever after.

Grade 11 – *Hoërskool Menlopark, Menlopark, Pretoria*

Be gentle on my mind

Ilan Chait

I have just enough time to polish off the luke-warm chicken pie and take a last sip of Coke before the bell begins its routine alarm. Swept along by the tide flowing down from the top field, I descend to the quad, where everyone darts off in different directions like fish dodging an underwater video camera.

The journey to the end of the earth gets under way. In the top corridor I'm again submerged in the sea of torsos. I remember the oral that is due and briefly feel my pocket for the clump of call cards that *should* be there. But there is no bump. A whining electric pulse begins to ripple through my body. Muscles tense, arteries contract. I force my left hand to check my other pocket, but with the same result. The memory which my mind so furiously tries to lock out is beginning to return. The foggy picture begins to clear, revealing the small, neat pile ... at home, on my bedside table.

I head for the back desk, centre row. She'll never see me. I sit down and calmly arrange my stationery in front of me. My trembling fingers fumble for my spectacles in my lapel. Wherever I look there are open mouths with words spilling out of them. Each person in his own world, reciting precious lines over and over. She has not yet arrived and it's already two minutes after the bell. Could she be absent, sick? Maybe car trouble? Never, not on a day like this.

My brain starts racing; the violent throbbing of my heart against my chest adds to my discomfort.

Everyone, startled by something, quickly scrambles. This can only mean one thing. Suddenly I spot her head gliding gracefully across the window sill. Her hair, glistening in the morning sun, is deadly. As she enters the classroom, my heavy body rises and my face returns her evil grin. She quickly dispenses with the formalities and exchanges pleasantries.

My body, which is now rigid like a brick, drops back into the cast-iron desk. The baritone hum that filled the room is replaced with cold, heavy silence. The first victim rises briskly and moves to the front. The words flow effortlessly, and she relishes every word. In a flash it is over. I can hear the soft scratching of her lead pencil on the paper as she writes her reward.

No one could ever have prepared me for what was about to happen next: I look up and my eyes clash with hers. Her pouting red lips arrange themselves into one of those your-turn smiles. The blood in my veins comes to a halt. Everything is still, as her stare jabs my gut. Her pupils, like pin-heads, remain fixed on mine.

"Ilan, wil jy jou toespraak nou kom hou?"

Her question remains unanswered.

I sit there cold, my mind not racing any more because this is the end. My head deflates like a leaking balloon, and the last thought seeping out of my skull is – *Be gentle on my mind, please do be gentle, soft.*

Grade 11 – *King David High, Linden, Jhb*

I find the commitment and limits of exams more daunting than the thought of looking down the barrel of a hijacker's gun. Examination time-limits frighten me, erase from my memory the long-studied syllabus and leave me numb. My hands tremble and my heart palpitates – even now as I merely contemplate this hideous scenario.

Danielle Levin
Grade 11 – King David High, Linden, Jhb

A prison for my soul
Rachel Grace van Vuuren

I am frightened out of my sleep by an insistent screaming in my ears. I am so used to it already, it just makes me feel despondent and paralysed. Why don't I throw the alarm clock out of the window, turn around and sleep another hour or so? It's so cosy here under my synthetic orange blanket and so chilly out there.

Five minutes later I put on my strict blue uniform while the snow is lying on the mountains like icing sugar and a biting wind is blowing. My eyes are heavy and constantly look down at my legs as I buckle up my black leather shoes. These legs make me think of that queer-looking George Michael's trendy stubble. Hell, I really don't feel like shaving. But people will stare and say ugly things about me. So I shave my legs.

I eat a slice of dry toast in the kitchen. The sun peeps at me through the window that faces east. I am ravenously hungry and I know my stomach is going to rumble for the rest of the day, but people look down on those who have some extra padding around the waste, even if they have just made the grade themselves.

I walk up the hill towards school in the early-morning air. Far away, I see the green mountains and the white snow now half-hiding under a light blanket of mist. Oh, to climb the mountain now and, for the first time, feel the soft snow melt and afterwards bask in the weak winter sun for the whole day! No, I have to go to school. If I don't go to school I will never get work so that I can buy a house and look after a family and pay for my own gravestone.

I go to school. Here everybody expects me to act lively, but this morning I got out on the wrong side of the bed. I have nothing against anyone. I just don't want to talk or smile. I walk past a familiar stranger and smile broadly, but my eyes don't laugh along.

It's the sixth period and by this time one just wants to go to sleep. Why don't I lie here on my graffiti-decorated desk with my arms under my head and build castles in the air? Magic castles with dove-grey and pink bricks, in a fairy-tale world without any evil fairies? The one in front stares at me through round frames. I quickly start working before she bewitches us with more homework. She just never stops.

The bell. We have to change classes. There's chaos in the crammed passages again. Just look at that kid with his ripe pimples and hyena smile in that yellow-and-pink colour scheme. He irritates me immeasurably. He is always in the way. I would like to give him a push (a light one, of course). Probably not worth it if he loses his cool?

"Hey, have you heard what happened last night at the hotel, in the jacuzzi?" And then you hear it. Blah-blah-blah. I just want to say: "Shut up!" but it's impolite and they will get angry. And I will reveal my personal preferences if I have to tell them why I don't mind certain people doing it behind glass sliding-doors. So I just pretend that I am busy digging for wax in both ears and dreadfully slowly hum the tune of a love song currently on the Top Ten.

At home everything is just too much. I've got to do something. Who cares what the neighbours think? Stirrers. I know! I'll turn the volume up and pretend that I am the lead singer in a heavy-metal rock group and scream out my lungs. The Alanis Morissette CD, her music is cool!

But if people hear me scream and find out that I have no reason to scream, they'll be angry.

They won't understand.

Maybe I should just shout so that only I can hear.

Silently.

Grade 11 – *Swellendam Hoërskool, Swellendam*

Igsaan Barendse – Battswood Art Centre

Misty water-coloured memories
Sanel van Wyk

"Oh no, not again," my tortured mind screams. "Please, stop, please," I whimper. But my pitiful pleas fall on deaf ears. He's appeared again – the small, furry, green and beady-eyed man. At least, that's what I think he is. He never comes close enough for me to get a good look at him. He's always in the corner, just sitting there staring, staring. Sometimes he keels over, face down, and then I'm free. Free from the prison of his gaze. Free from his condemning eyes which follow me everywhere, at all times.

But just when I think I'm free – THEY come. I never see their faces clearly. In fact, they look like some cliché of a ghost – all in white, with black, hollow eyes. They always wake up the little man. And the torture begins again, the sit-and-stare torture. I've tried to fight him a number of times, tried to get him to stop. But even when I've thrashed and beaten him up, and I look at him lying on the floor, his eyes keep accusing me. Tormenting me.

I cannot remember where he came from, but something tells me I used to love him, my beady-eyed "friend". I can sometimes see a painful look of longing in his eyes. It puzzles me, though I somehow know I'm supposed to understand why he longs and what he longs for. Somewhere among the cobwebs of my memory, I see myself playing in a garden among masses of rainbow-coloured flowers. The girl who's me has happy brown eyes and shiny jet-black hair and the sun is making my cheeks glow. Beady is in my arms and I'm laughing. I don't know why, but it seems natural.

Suddenly a woman and a man approach me. A cloud blocks out my sunshine and I know it's time. Time for what …? I don't feel good any longer. I clutch onto Beady as the man and woman lead me into the small dark room at the back of the yard. Somehow I know I've been taken there before. We approach the small dark room with the black wooden door. The place is evil and threatening.

A scream shatters the silence of the scene I have been observing at the back of my mind, like a silent movie. The scream is ear-shattering. At first it sounds like it's a thousand miles away but then I realise it's me who's screaming. I can see the horrible picture of the nightmare I'm going to experience. I *know* what's going to happen.

"NO! NO! I don't want to see, don't want to remember!"

Tears come streaming down my cheeks, my heart is pounding desperately as I try to lock away that painful memory, to continue the fight between remembering and trying to forget. But to no avail. The picture keeps returning. I can hear the man and the woman talking, but it doesn't make any sense to me. All I know is that they are going to hurt me. First the man and then the woman. I feel my body stiffen and a cold shiver runs up my spine as I endure the torture of abuse for the umpteenth time …

I open my eyes and look up at the white ceiling. Not a stain on it – so pure. I rub my eyes, they are wet with tears. I must have been crying – but why?

I'm filled with a sudden rage, so intense that it blots out all other emotions. I feel so angry – but I don't know why. I get off my bed and my eyes fall on Beady. As if driven by a force from hell, I pick up Beady, rip off his arms and legs and pound his head with my fists until those damning eyes of his pop out. I want to destroy everything. I want to kill. Why? Because of that man and that woman – Daddy and Mommy!

I sweep everything off my dresser and laugh wildly as I hear my glass ornaments crash to the floor.

I catch a glimpse of my face in the mirror and I hate it. So I pound with my fists against the mirror, hardly feeling the pain from the glass cutting into my hands …

My door bursts open and two men come rushing in. They try to calm me but can't. One has a needle in his hand, and while the other holds my writhing body down, he injects me. I feel a numbness taking over my brain, my body. I hear one of them saying, "Worst case of abuse I've ever seen. Poor girl, only nine years old and already in a madhouse. Killed her parents. With a pair of scissors, in their sleep …"

Grade 12 – *Mmabatho High, Mmabatho*

The interview
Brandon Horwitz

HE peers into his stellar larder and sees the galaxies pirouette and cavort in their usual fashion. HE sights a star. It returns his gaze, neither imploring to be chosen nor seeking anonymity. HE is fascinated by its indifference, and has it brought before him.

"I will give you life – will you take it?"
"I … I don't know, what is it like?"
"There is good; there is bad."
"What is good?"
"Good is devotion. You will feel a mother's arms enfolding you, she will suckle you, she will rear you. Your life will be her life and you will feel acceptance, you will feel warmth, you will not fear. You will learn of friendship, of bonds between you and others, bonds more steadfast than steel, bonds encircling your life, pervading all and lending light to everything they touch. This is good.
"The mother will forget you, you will suck and the teat will be dry, you will seek guidance and will receive apathy. Your life will be nothing and you will feel abandonment, you will feel the whip of winter, you will fear. From friendship you will learn of betrayal, the facet of life which pervades all and leaves few unsullied. This, too, is good."
"That, too, is good? What then is bad?"
"Much, but don't worry, there is more good. Good is choice. You will not be able to draw breath without some decision needing your attention: whom to help, what to create, when to rejoice. In the choice is power, the power to build and the power to give. This is good.
"Neither will you be able to draw breath without some temptation demanding your weakness: whom to injure, what to destroy, when to despair. In choice is power, the power to demolish and the power to take. Doubtless, this, too, is good."
"It is? But if this, too, is good, what then is left to be bad?"
"Fear not, of bad there is plenty. Of good, scant more!
"Good is experience. Love will find you, as will her bridesmaids, Joy and Contentment. You will taste knowledge in all its splendour and discover philosophy and learning. Through ambition you will feel achievement, and in application you will find pride. Such experiences may

darken your life and the lives around you. But remember, this, too, is good."

"This is good, despite appearing bad?"

"It is."

"How can that be? And then, what *is* bad?"

"Would you really like to know what is bad?"

"Yes."

"If you can do anything in life, it is good, even doing nothing in life is good."

"Yes, yes, so what is bad?"

"Bad is when I call you back."

Grade 12 – King David High, Linden, Jhb

Most human beings spend their days thinking and dreaming about where they are *not*. To be effective in our lives, we must develop the art of living in the place where we are standing and at the moment we're in.

Dora Fiona Francis
Grade 12 – St Boniface High, Kimberley

Waleed Hendricks – Battswood Art Centre

Wallflowers
Joanne Hobbs

A gust of cool air, tainted with the cloying scent of attar of roses, announced her arrival. I looked up from where I was reviewing my list of clients on that cool April day and smiled.

"May I help you?" I asked.

Only then did I notice her striking appearance. Hair black as a raven's wing cascaded over her shoulders to her waist. A skunk streak of pure silver ran through it. She was small and trim, dressed in a jet-black suit and – strangely – a pair of delicate lace gloves. Most striking were her ice-blue eyes. Eyes that sent chills up and down my spine.

"Yes, I believe you can." Her voice was low, husky. "Unless you *aren't* Doctor Leibman …?" She laughed, probably realising that this was not an uncommon name, especially not in the medical fraternity, and added: " … the psychiatrist?"

I smiled again, politely. "Yes, I am. But who are you?"

"Why, I'm Lily Constantine." She obviously expected a reaction, but I had not the remotest idea who she was. She sighed at my ignorance. "I'm an artist, a sculptor. I specialise in ethnic art. But people usually remember me for my death masks."

"Well!" I exclaimed. "Would you like to come into my office?" I opened the door and gestured to her to precede me. She sat down in the chair facing my desk. "Shall we get down to business?"

She nodded slightly and I asked her what she would like to talk about.

"Well, you see, something has been bothering me lately. It's something from my past. I was sixteen when it happened." She looked out of the window, her eyes taking on a glazed, distant look. Was she looking at something she had long thought buried? Something that would be as unpleasant to exhume as an old corpse?

Sighing, she turned back to me. "I have a younger brother and sister – twins, Owen and Belinda. They have been in a home for the … disturbed, since they were five. That would mean they have been there for …" She bit her lip, considering this. "Oh, twenty years it would be."

I broke one of my rules and interrupted her. "Of course this must be disturbing to you. Anyone would find it troubling, but after all these …"

Her icy gaze brought me up short. I coughed and apologised for the interruption.

She continued. "I was sixteen, they were five. My parents were cold people, at least they were with me. But not with Owen and Belinda. No, they were their 'darlings', their 'cherubs'."

Her voice was twisting with anger and bitterness. I had seen this before; it was what I call the snake-eating-its-own-tail syndrome. Children who hate their parents because of their coldness and aloofness, still seem to think that the fault is actually their own, that in their earlier childhood they had done something bad though they cannot remember it.

"Don't get the wrong idea, I love O and Bee. It's my parents that I *hated*. Obviously, there were others who disliked them even more than I did. You see, my parents were murdered." She looked up to gauge my reaction. I merely nodded.

"I was the first to discover their bodies. They had been stabbed to death, my father first. He was still lying on the bed. Then Mother. She had tried to get away. She was on the floor, the stab-wounds inflicted from behind. They had their eyes open, so they knew what had happened to them." To this day I believe that she smiled at that thought. Still more frightening was the way in which she described it: coldly, clinically, with deadly calm.

"But Doctor, they were not alone. My brother and sister were sitting on the floor of their room, the knife between them, painting flowers on each other's cheeks. *They* were the ones who had killed my parents, or so the police said. *Their* fingerprints were on the knife and there was no evidence of a break-in."

She rose with a graceful, fluid motion, then walked over to the wall and ran one hand over it. "This reminds me of their wallpaper. The same little red flowers. The blood just seemed a lovely addition. The dark red of the flowers off-set by the crimson droplets."

I shuddered, horror welling up.

"This is in the strictest of confidence, isn't it? The attorney-client privilege sort of thing."

"Yes," I managed to utter.

She nodded, satisfied. Then softly, "There's a line in Cervantes's *Don Quixote* which I always thought applied to me: 'I shall be as secret as the grave.' And I was, you know, up to now." Then she giggled; all solemnity vanished. "You see, my good Doctor, Owen and Belinda had nothing to do with the … *murder*. NO! That's not the right word! Shall we call it *justice*? Albeit vigilante. Yes, that seems right. Justice." She seemed to taste the word and found it to her liking.

Sighing, she said, "I do regret having had to use O and Bee, but it was for the greater good. *Mine!*" She cackled, taking off her gloves as she approached my desk. She stuck out one hand. "As you can see, that night left its mark on me." Her delicate palm was cruelly scarred.

"You wouldn't believe how gullible the police can be! Turn on the water works and they believe you're innocent. 'Officer, I tried to get the knife away from them and they slashed my hand in the process!'" Her voice had reached the high pitch of hysteria. Then she smiled again, all traces of hysteria vanishing as abruptly as they had appeared.

"Well, Doctor," she said in a brisk tone now, "I must be off. Thank you for listening." She said this as though she had told me a mere bagatelle.

I sat at my desk; numb, incapable of movement. She reached across my desk and patted my hand. "Now, now, it's not as bad as all that" – as though she were consoling a child.

"You *do* have a gift for understatement!" was the only thought that crossed my mind.

She turned and walked out, leaving the way she had come in: accompanied by a cool gust of air tainted by the cloying scent of attar of roses.

A scent reminiscent of death …

Grade 12 – *Holy Rosary, Edenvale*

Only sixteen
Thomas Cox

Bullets and blood. I'm only sixteen. A broken mirror and a silver straw, these are my toys. They say I am a child. Barely sixteen, I've sold my soul, my life, my dreams. I do not own, I'm merely possessed. White powder my master, cold steel my answer. Only a child? I'm crumpled and tired. I've slept in a gutter, my nose is bleeding. Sixteen, and looking back only.

Yes, I look back but it's too late. Over my shoulder the world is the same. It is I who have changed ...

Fourteen years old – wow, that's cool. I'm dizzy and sick. It took two days to come back but I was taken – give me some more!

Thirteen years now and looking for fun. Her name is Ashley. She says it is normal. I think I'm in love.

Ten years old. I'm a big boy now.

Six years, and I'm a ninja turtle. I play toy cars. I'll be a policeman when I'm big.

Three years old, the world is so new. I hide behind my mother's skirts.

One year old and I'm learning to talk.

Ten seconds old and I'm crying. Should I have been born at all?

This is my life. It seems so short, I feel so old. Mom, Dad, I wonder if you know. I died in your eyes a long time ago, I died with my lies.

The barrel of a gun looms familiarly. The TV glows and hisses. Why bother to tune it? The radio shrieks. My head is aching. But there's nothing to turn off.

The gun lies smoking on the floor, fallen from my hand. I lie unmoving, entwined in the darkness of my lover.

Grade 11 – *St Stithians College, Randburg*

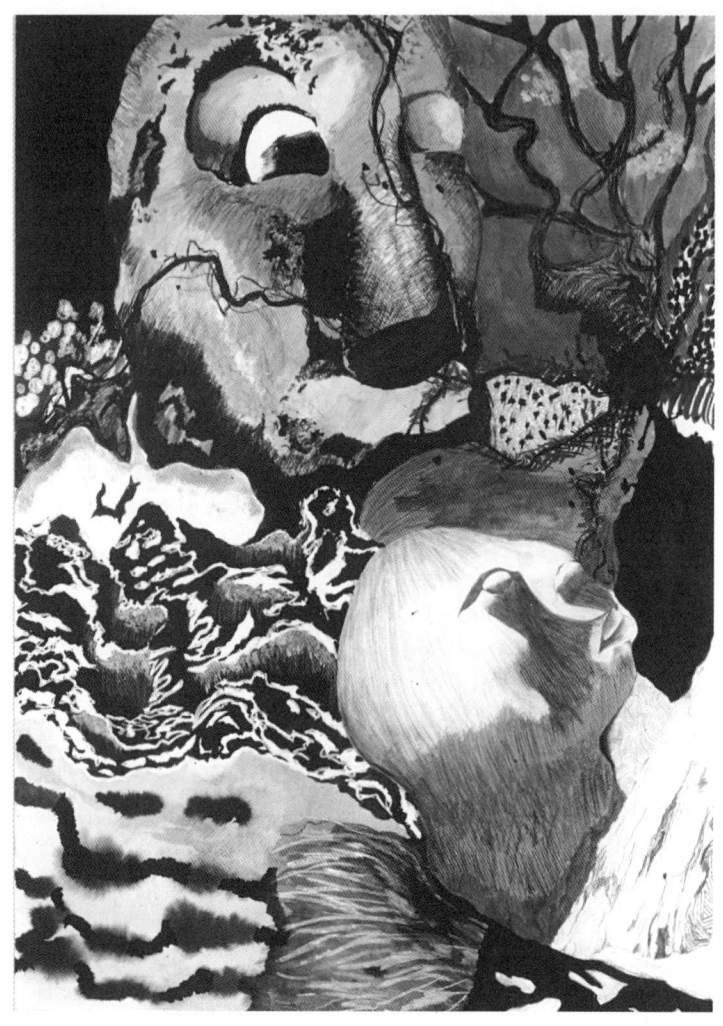

Thando Koda – Frank Joubert Art Centre

Locked away
Liron Meister

The door is shut. The lock is automatically activated. The air conditioner quietly pumps a chilly breeze into the interior. The metal capsule is transformed into a tank – German engineering when you need it most. The towering walls of our mansion grow bigger as the vehicle approaches. The heavy metal gate squeaks to provide the smallest possible exit. As the car accelerates, the chains tighten on the freedom I dare not enjoy.

The windows remain shut; the temptation to breathe fresh air has long since vanished. I finger the electronic switch but lack the courage to exert pressure on it. I realise that the slightest opening could become a life-threatening risk. I fear the tools of violence that have seized control of my existence: the knife, the gun, the axe.

Fear has infected the whole nation – the country has contracted an uncontrollable disease.

I inhabit a fortress. The shadow of steel bars appears on the floors when the curtains are drawn, and the sun struggles to shine through. The towering walls, topped with high-tension wiring, imprison me. Electronic gates and metal locks secure the entrances. My home is only one of countless cells that have transformed our neighbourhood into a prison.

Stories of hijackings, robberies, rapes and murders confine me to my cell. Keep alert! Lock the door! Seal the windows! These obsessional routines have isolated me from society. I have immunised myself to this horrific environment but at what cost?

Members of my family compulsively hide their possessions in the most sophisticated safes. Any sign of luxury is an invitation to a burglar.

The shackles of violence have created an atmosphere of terror and so our life has become unbearable. As I sit in my cage, I wonder if these shackles can ever be broken or if we will remain voluntary captives for the rest of our lives.

Grade 12 – *King David High, Linden, Jhb*

These things happen
Julia Smuts Louw

Mrs Khumalo?
Mrs George Khumalo?
Could we step inside?
We are sorry to have to inform you …
> *no thank you*

that regrettably we must tell you …
> *you'd better sit down, Mrs Khumalo*

We are sorry to have to inform you
that regrettably we must tell you
that it is our unpleasant duty
to report the news
that your husband
was shot dead …
twice, in the head …
on the corner of Park and Jameson
at 8 o'clock this morning.
Nobody's fault, Mrs Khumalo
> *especially not ours*

You will forgive us if we leave now
> *duty calls*

You will forgive us if we leave now
> *before your numbness*
> *splinters into realisation –*
> *how awkward that would be*

You will forgive us
if we leave
> *feet shuffling*
> *heads bowed and wagging*
> *eyes full of*
> *guilt? grief?*
> *compassion? relief?*

Our condolences, Mrs Khumalo.
These things happen …
> *just not to us*

Grade 11 – *Herschel, Claremont*

On my way home
Ivor Petersen

Purposefully putting one foot in front of the other, I walk along the shining darkness of the rough tar. It has just rained and a thin layer of moisture lies on the road. This additional little pleasure, after a late night with my friends, makes my blood run strongly.

Tonight, once more, I have to take on the dangers of the Cape Flats on my way home. My fateful route takes me along various paths through Bonteheuwel – or Bontas as it is known. Here and there a damaged street lamp flickers listlessly like a dying star and I surrender myself to the heavy, unusual silence that guides me through this concrete jungle.

But it's only a fleeting illusion. Thank goodness, for a moment I was feeling like one of those upper-class dreamers. Two shots resound, enough to jerk me back into reality. At least they sound far away enough and I am not in immediate danger. Out of habit I feel for the protective, reassuring hardness of my knife. I am not a gangster, in a jungle, however, survival is a priority. It's funny, but three years ago I would have confused those shots with the back-firing of a rusty jalopy. Now shots in the night are a common, almost non-fazing reality.

I walk a little faster. It is raining harder. The street lamps appear even duller. The wetness starts to stick to me irritatingly. Lucky that it was only two shots. On Sunday night six shots had sounded monotonously and rhythmically somewhere in the darkness and had pierced some or other stupid body, monotonously and rhythmically. It had sounded like crackers on a cheery New Year's Eve. If only it had been that!

I am running, panting. My chest is burning. I'm soaked by the drizzle. My need for reassurance makes me reach for the knife again. Why is the blade open? I look back, slightly confused. Under the flickering street lamp I see a shuddering shadow. The moans of a child are muted by my wheezy panting. I increase my speed. My blade is still open and wet. Like an animal in the jungle, I run home, confused. From street, to street, to street.

I pluck open the front door. Somebody is hysterical. Our house feels strange. Someone is crying.

I stand confused before my parents. My father is holding my frightened mother and looks at me with empty, ghostlike eyes. He turns into a pillar of salt in front of me.

Finally my mother looks up and between deep, choking sobs she murmurs slowly and painfully: "We have just heard. Your brother was ... he was shot dead. Two shots."

Grade 12 – Jan van Riebeeck, Cape Town

Chains
Sharon Radebe

The chains on the gate secure me. Their rust is like a stamp of safety. The chains on my mind restrain me. Like a semi-permeable cell wall they only allow certain thoughts to pass through. The chains in my heart bond me to those I love, ensuring lasting togetherness.

But chains can be broken.

A family holiday was severed by a phone call reporting an attempted burglary at our house. The smashed pieces of glass on the floor betrayed the thief's urge to possess our Panasonic appliance. The clang of the security gate against the frame of the sliding door told its story of defeat. The chain on the door hung in shame.

Fear gripped and throttled me. The realisation that no number of chains on the doors can keep out a committed criminal punched my mind like an ungloved fist. A burglar is driven by stronger forces than morality, decency or kindness; his motivation is cold, hunger and violent greed.

The desperation behind his act makes me doubt the security of the chains on my gates. They hang limply like dead snakes, pretending to be on guard. The wickedness of his act weakens the chains in my mind that guard me from the debilitating fear of losing my family in a violent way. The clinical routine with which the crime was executed corrodes the chains in my heart that bond me to the ones I love.

The violation of my home leaves me feeling naked and vulnerable. Sadly, I have to accept that alarms cannot stop a gun; Quantas cannot curb danger; fences cannot stop a robber; nor can chains prevent a murder.

The only protection I have is the bond with my family, friends and neighbours. The closeness that we share comforts us in times of uncertainty like these. It covers me with a warm blanket more secure than any wall or chain can ever be.

Grade 12 – King David High, Linden, Jhb

"As long as crime doesn't affect or harm me, I'm OK," said a friend of mine the other day. But is that acceptable? I have twice seen Mr Nelson Mandela pleading on TV with our young educated people not to leave this country. Why are they leaving? One reason is that they want safety. They don't want to be scared to walk down a dark street or go to an ATM machine. They want freedom, and currently South Africa cannot guarantee their freedom.

Yuval Abraham
Grade 11 – Westerford High, Rondebosch, Cape

Self-portrait
Danielle Levin

Look into the mirror. Look very carefully at yourself. Do not stand so close that you lose your focus. Take a step back and absorb the overall picture. I do not think that you will like what you see. No, I do not mean the salon-styled hair or the flawlessly blended skin or the glossy red lips. Look at your eyes: they are glazed with lifelessness.

You are a perfect product of your environment and upbringing. Your parents primed you from the start to achieve what they failed to accomplish. This is the most unenviable task I can think of. It is not surprising that you are weary and worn out. You dare not fail your parents after all the money they have invested in you and the precious time they have spent on you. All you had to do was to give up your individuality and happiness.

Now look into the mirror and say whether it was worth achieving their elusive aims.

I know that sometimes you have a selfish attitude and think that you deserve to take all decisions that affect your life. Forget about any such thoughts. You are young and possess a quaint naïveté that will get you nowhere. You are not competent to pass your own judgement. You must accept this fact completely in order to avoid disappointment. When you are more capable and experienced you will appreciate the choices that have been made for you.

Stop wanting to break free and leap out of the family portrait into your own frame. You must want to be what they expect, rather than what you feel deep within. Feelings like these are childlike and idealistic and have no place in an economically orientated adult world. Affluence, power, status: these are all of paramount importance; morality is expendable. Do not ask questions.

The only alternative is to waste your life, living in "artistic" squalor. But only a fool would jeopardise a cosy future for a whim; such spontaneity leads only to regret.

By now you have probably considered all your options or lack thereof and realised that you have to betray your parents to stay true to yourself.

I suggest you take a large blunt object and hurl it at the mirror.

Grade 11 – *King David High, Linden, Jhb*

Andrea Gordon – Battswood Art Centre

You sometimes experience a moment of resistance, resentment or fear when confronted with your hidden self. But if this happens you should be happy, for this is the only path to renewal of yourself.

David Fikile Kanguwe
Grade 11 – *St Boniface High, Kimberley*

The telephone conversation
Renél Espag

Slowly, slowly, like a tortoise, I tighten my grip on the receiver. It feels like an elongated block of lead which I, with all my strength, try to bring to my ear, until it is finally pressed hard against my head.

I lick my dry lips. My heartbeat is racing through my throat, right up against my ear and I can hardly hear the dialling tone. I breathe deeply and heavily and I constantly swallow nervously.

The index finger on my right hand shakes like that of an old woman's while it runs through the first few entries of Van Wyk. Down, down until it stops at Van Wyk, R J, 17 Albatross Ave, Walmer. Slowly but surely I drag my finger along the dotted line to the right of the phone book where the numbers are.

Your number.

A few seconds later I stare at it. My body feels lame. Tentatively I press the numbers. First a four, then an eight, a three and again a four with a nine and a two.

I wait.

The phone rings three, four times, prr, prr, prr, prr ... until I hear your voice as clear as a bell on a cool winter evening. Your greeting echoes in my ears like a mountain thrush. I quickly put down the receiver.

Flustered, I swallow again. Your voice is all I wanted to hear, all I can cope with.

Tomorrow I shall phone again.

Grade 11 – *Hoërskool D F Malherbe, Walmer*

Mr Hangman
Louise Crouse

"Are you ready, Mr Ward?"

"As ready as I will ever be," answered the old man without a trace of fear in his eyes. "But the question is, are *you* ready?"

The young man managed to lock the hand-cuffs only after the second attempt. "It is eleven forty-five," he said hastily and almost inaudibly. "Time to walk."

"Am I right in saying that this is the first time that you are leading a condemned man to his death?" asked the prisoner calmly. Much too calmly for someone who knew that he was taking his last steps. "You can answer me, Mr Hangman. Don't feel guilty about my lot. And don't ignore me either. Allow me my last conversation."

"What makes you think that this is my first time, Mr Ward?" came the indignant answer, almost like that of a boy whose secret had been revealed.

"Come, come! Let's drop the formalities. Just call me Jack. It is your bearing which betrays your ignorance, Mr Hangman. You are inexperienced in this game, not so? Come, come! You tremble even worse than I do."

"You are right … Jack. I am inexperienced. But this is definitely not my first time, and I'm thoroughly aware that I'm trembling. If the situation wasn't so serious it would probably be funny," he stuttered.

"Ironic, hey? Very ironic," Jack whispered thoughtfully. He looked ahead, his eyes misty, unaware of the hands stretched out towards him, unaware of the other prisoners shouting at him. He walked as if he were going for a stroll, but he knew that they knew.

"What do you mean, Jack?"

"Somewhere I read that young men who are condemned to death turn grey during their final walk," he said. "Have you come across this yet in your short career as a hangman? They say it's because of the enormous tension suffered by men who are condemned to death. They literally walk to their death."

Jack spoke fast and sounded confident. "Well, I have been grey for a long time," he continued. "Long before I was found guilty. Do you think, Mr Hangman, that hangmen also turn grey from doing their work?"

"I have not experienced it yet, but I have heard stories about this," the hangman said thoughtfully.

"Murderers have been taken along this passage in wheel chairs, others were dragged ... or so I hear. You are probably glad that you don't have any problems with me, Mr Hangman. Tell me, how does it feel to lead someone to his death? Do you feel that you have the power to end someone's life legally? Tell me, Hangman, does it make you feel powerful?"

Jack's eyes seemed to look straight through him.

"No!" The hangman was getting flustered. "I hate this work. But someone has to do it and I need the money. I feel as if I will never get used to executing criminals. I hate it!" he shouted in despair.

"Strange that you should experience it like that. It didn't take me long to get used to this routine. You see, I have walked this path more than once ..."

Grade 12 – *Langenhoven Gimnasium, Oudtshoorn*

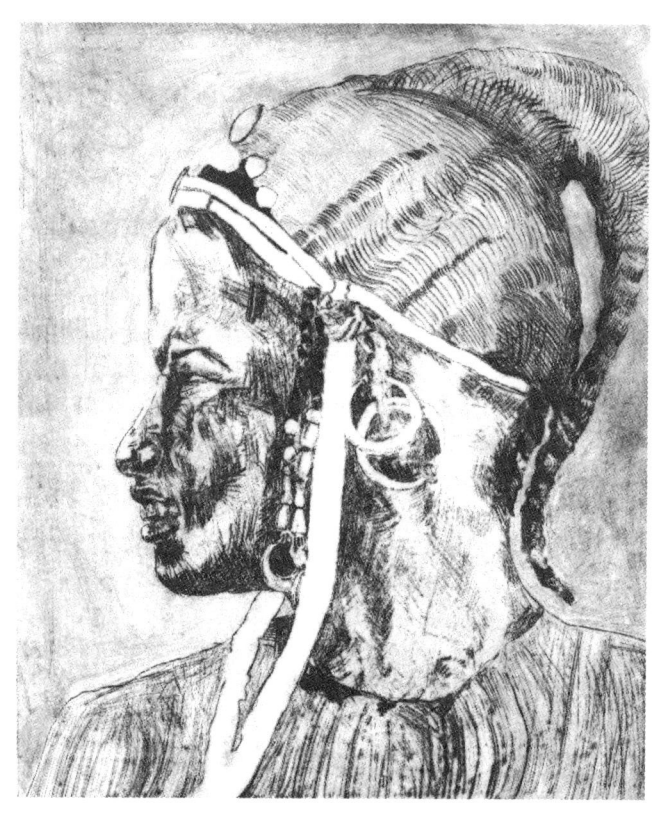

Camilla Fraser – Frank Joubert Art Centre

Thirteen steps
Ezanne Jordaan

In the early hours, while life was still awakening, and the sun lay hidden behind the mountain, a small boy was walking up the hill with his father. His hand was folded into his father's. But his father's hand was heavy and clumsy. He was caught in the web of his thoughts.

The little boy's foot hooked in something and he fell onto his knees between the cold rocks. He looked up and it seemed as if his father's strides were growing longer and longer. Confused, he ran after him. When he caught up with him, he was out of breath and pushed his little hand back into the cold, hard one.

They reached the top of a cliff. The cold hand tightened its grip and suddenly sent him to the edge. The little boy pulled back, frightened, but his father's rough hand jerked him forward. He threw him into the air and the boy was left to the mercy of an arc of strong muscles. He could feel for a moment how the dark was pulling him in, swallowing him, and he looked with bewildered eyes at the moon-face of his father. The muscles relaxed. His father's laughter roared above the echo. The next moment he pulled the boy tightly against his chest. The boy felt the sticky, wet hair on his father's chest and he knew that there were pearls of sweat on his father's forehead.

His father pushed him away and he felt his head jerk. He felt the grating breath against his neck and listened to his father breathlessly repeating their little secret game. It was as if these familiar words reassured the little boy and banished his fear. He did not understand his father's excitement, but he was overjoyed that he could share such a secret and that he could make his father feel proud of him.

His father gave him the yellow cloth and the little boy sat down on his haunches. Carefully, just as his father had taught him, he unfolded the soft corners of the cloth. Then he rested the heavy pistol his father had handed him, on it.

His father took a small box from his pocket and counted out six bullets. With practised fingers the little boy slid the bullets into their smooth tunnels and slided in the magazine, until he heard the click. Then he put the pistol on the ground and walked to his father with the turmeric-yellow cloth. His father bent forward. The boy tied the cloth over his eyes and carefully knotted it behind his head. Then he took his father's big hand, led him right to the edge of the cliff and left him there with his back to the precipice.

With the pistol in his hand the boy counted thirteen steps. It was his father's lucky number. Behind his father's dark figure he could see the rays of dawn. The child lifted both hands, aimed at the heart and pulled the trigger. He ran laughing to where his father had staggered back and vanished. But then he stopped. He remembered clearly how his father had hit him over the head the last time they had practised this on the balcony.

And so he turned around and walked down the hill, slowly, back in the direction of the house.

Under his father's beloved oak tree he buried the pistol and ran back to where his mother would soon wake up and get ready for church.

Over and over he repeated the incomprehensible little poem he had practised so many times with his father. Now he could recite it to his mother.

Grade 12 – *Hoër Meisieskool La Rochelle, Paarl*

Where the roads fork
Adèle Goligorsky

The night sidles away and the watery black sky dissolves into a twittering, delphinium-blue rhapsody. Blinking white and red advertisements shout into the silhouetted silence. Yesterday's laundry is a multicoloured assortment of flags flapping in the peppermint breeze.

In the east, dramatic shades of orange and yellow wrestle their way through the gaps between the tall, dark buildings. The west is a silky scarf draped over golden suburbs, crouching beneath less obstructed rays. In the far north there are hazy open spaces backed by watery mountains, and from my position the view of the south can only be imagined.

A grey dove rises from the shadows of building structures and a night watchman stumbles home wearily. A brown haze leaks out from a single chimney and mingles with the light to make an angry sky. It swirls against the walls of the maze that contains life.

We are the solvers of the puzzle of our lives. No two of us walk our paths in the same sequence nor do we see them in the same light. Those who have been there before us have changed them and those who will walk in the warmth of our footsteps will change them again. These lanes become memories and when we visit them, they are familiar, but always different.

I think of the space that used to be my home, where I said my first words, where I kept my first pet and even scribbled my five-times table with a blue crayon in the corner of a cupboard. The mail which is delivered there now bears another family's name, and they have long since painted over our personal marks and begun inscribing their own.

The nursery school I attended now buzzes with the laughter of strangers' children and the primary school where I spent the greater part of seven years now lies on someone else's path. The holiday camp which once seemed so big and imposing, now possesses a picturesque charm and has shrunk in the vortex of my memory. These places, as I remember them, exist only in photographs hanging on walls or pasted in the photo albums of those whose paths converged there and may cross again on their respective journeys.

However, in our random wanderings through the world's maze most of us are unlikely to meet again through the walls of security, reserve, fear and prejudice.

Every turn leads to a new series of turns and old options disappear forever. Occasionally we stop to gaze back to the fork where the roads diverged and agree with whoever said that it is a pity that we cannot travel both, and be one traveller.

As we are now, there is nowhere we can stand to view the maze in its entirety. Even from space, astronauts can see only a part of our great sphere at one time.

Most of us choose to peep around as many corners as we can. Occasionally we glance back at the scenes behind old, familiar corners where we consider ourselves secure. If we realise that these scenes have changed irrevocably, we venture around a new corner to face new challenges. Our minds wander up to the world's dreamy azure ceiling, sweetened by white marshmallow clouds shot with the glorious pink and orange shades of today's sunset. Together with the evening stars they float on the peppermint breeze and we follow them to a place from where we will witness a sunrise unlike any other that has touched the walls around us with warmth.

Grade 11 - Roedean, Parktown

Even in our present era when much has been done to emancipate the female gender socially, women are still not in total control over decisions about their own bodies. Although a woman may no longer be viewed simply as a "baby machine", she is now plagued by feelings of inadequacy as to her appearance. How often are we guilty of categorising a woman according to her physical attractiveness? An attractive woman may be spurned by members of her own sex, because she is seen as more likely to have successful relationships with men; so she is considered a threat to other women's relationships. Tragically, women have gone from being victims of male insecurity to becoming victims of their own insecurity.

Megan Jones
Grade 11 – Pietermaritzburg Girls' High, Pmb

Fatima Khan – Battswood Art Centre

In the dead of night
Novuyo Halimana

She was the sweetest lady in the village, it was said. It was also said of her – behind closed doors, of course – that she had "things". Tales that were brushed aside as old wives' tales, yet they robbed the villagers of their sleep in the dead of night.

Betty had a younger sister, Ruth. She had been given that name by the "man without knees", whose silhouette against the dying sun above the mountain still haunted the village like a curse.

Ruth had been blessed with a baby girl at the rising of the new full moon. The elderly women shook their grey heads sadly. "It is a bad omen, a bad omen," they muttered through decaying teeth.

But there was much rejoicing in Ruth's homestead, with home-brewed beer, music and dancing, and for a short while everyone seemed to forget their troubles. The villagers danced into the dead of night.

As was the custom, the royal messenger arrived with a pure white she-goat – a symbol of purity, womanhood, fertility.

Betty, who had remained unmarried, had never experienced the sweetness, pride and honour of being a mother. While Ruth was serving refreshments to the guests, Betty held the baby close to her bosom – a bosom cold and dark as night. She muttered something under her breath, again and again, louder and louder till the baby sneezed as if in response. Betty smiled triumphantly and returned her niece to her mother, who accepted the tiny baby with the pride of a queen yet the humbleness of a lamb.

As the moon rose to its throne it seemed to light up the mountain. Then there was a shrill scream, "The shrine, the shrine must not be burnt!" And soon the town was cleared of all its able-bodied men, who went to fight the fire on the mountain.

In the ensuing commotion no one saw IT enter Ruth's house and no one saw IT leave. If the wind had not swept away ITs footprints, they would have been seen leading right up to Betty's door.

Ruth and her child were buried by the villagers. A week after the fire their bodies were no more – and the village was strangely quiet. Except for the hyenas calling to their mistress for more food in the dead of night.

Ruth's spirit reappeared: After nine moons three households were presented with baby girls. One of them did not live to see her first sunrise. The second one survived. Her mother had been purified by the rainmaker. And the last one disappeared during the night of the new moon. She was never found.

One day, the rainmaker came back to the village. She said that the spirits of the dead were wailing, that the evil force that had silenced their bodies could not put their souls to rest.

"The soil of this village is drenched with the blood of the living dead," the rainmaker said in her deep, grave voice.

The only way the village could be purified, so the spirits had said, was for the whole village to be "washed". This cleansing was to be done in the very dead of night while the people slept.

It happened as the spirits had said.

A drizzle mixed with the early morning smoke and spread a filthy, dark blanket over the village. As the sun came up, the fog cleared to reveal blackness and death. Among the smouldering huts in the village centre a naked black hump moved. The claw of a hyena was tied with a thread around ITS neck.

A pack of hyenas circled closer and closer about the village as they smelled food …

By dusk of that long day, Betty's body was no more, and the hyenas cackled triumphantly as they slunk off into the dead of night.

Grade 12 – *Mmabatho High, Mmabatho*

The adventures of a wild Afrikaner-wannabe
(with apologies to Danie)

Michelle Matthews

He sucks on his pipe as if it were his breath and closes his eyes with the self-satisfaction of an infant. Then he leans back against the wall and nurses the broken bottleneck between his hands.

"Last week I went to OK Bazaars, and hell, the price of toilet paper is ridiculous."

Everybody just nods. They know that he is tired, ag hell, that he is *gatvol*. He's already exhausted all the psychiatrists. The first one terminated his career and is writing a novel. The second one sold all his possessions and moved to who knows where. The third one apparently committed suicide.

"Where's my Tassies?" he suddenly asks.

"Between your legs," I say.

He looks mournfully at the green bottle. "Darling, you know I love you, but I would feel much more turned on if you were a bottle of whiskey." He takes a sip in any case.

"Tastes like honey," somebody sings slightly off-key and some people giggle. Everybody is smoked up by now.

He holds the bottle towards me. I sit closest to him. Suddenly I sharply remember sour vomit, looking like clotted blood.

"No thanks," I say.

"You know," he leans forward and stares at me intensely, one eye closed. "You're actually ugly." And then with a lewd grin: "But you have a wonderful voice."

I smile at him.

"I'm gonna have a braai for some friends tonight. Lucky you – you are invited."

He throws his head back and the wine gargles into his body. He breaks the empty bottle and gets up.

"Come, I'm driving."

Arriving at his home, all I can think about is getting to the toilet.

"Around the corner, first door left."

As I close the door I feel as if I'm locked in. The tiles date from the seventies, those ugly, shiny orange-brown ones. On the floor are a few Bitterkomix copies and I wonder whether they have to serve as toilet paper. I fumble around, embarrassed. Without toilet paper in a stranger's house! As I turn around panic-stricken, I get a huge fright. On top of the cistern sits an ugly, pink poodle, one of those knitted ones with tassels. A good example of Afrikaner kitsch or what? Or is it a joke? You never know with alternative Afrikaans poets!

"Okay, cavity search!" I shout at the pooch and pull out its innards.

There are a few people in the sitting room. My host is reclining on a dirty couch. A plumpish red-head with a neon-orange dress and fifties' glasses sits on his lap. His hand is on her thigh and she tells him a joke about a police dog and Nietzsche. Ha-ha-ha!

In the corner is one of those couch-cum-bed things. It is open. A young guy lies on it with his arms above his head. His little Go-Go Girl shirt is pulled up so that I can see his smooth stomach above his colourful bell-bottoms. He strokes the bed next to him. "Come and lie here, sister."

I go and sit next to him. He looks straight at me with his bright brown eyes that carry a gleam of laughter. "Lie down, sister."

I collapse uncomfortably. A thin Coloured guy with bleached blond hair sits on the farthest corner of the bed and crumbles hashish into last Tuesday's edition of Die Burger. He doesn't look up. "Are you flirting with the girls again, darling?" he says to the guy on the bed.

Go-go Girl laughs out loud. "Jealous!" he crows. "Oh, don't worry, I'm just playing with her."

The Coloured guy looks at him admonishingly and Go-Go Girl blows him a little kiss. Our poetic host and his girl come over.

"How are things?" he asks the man on the corner of the bed.

"Nearly ready," he answers, while he rolls out his Rizzlas.

"And how are you?" He turns towards me.

"Very well, thank you," I say shyly.

"Hey," screams Go-Go Girl, "she's English!"

And I blush.

"What are you actually doing here among us rock-spiders?" asks Go-Go Girl.

"Well," I stutter, "I … ugh … well." I'm so scared that I'll make a fool of myself. "It's just like it says on the cover of Bitterkomix No. 6 …"

Everybody looks at me as if I were saying something really weird. "I mean ... 'Afrikaners is plesierig'. You know, like in that old song of yours."

Apparently this statement is very funny.

"She sounds just like out of *Afrikaans my taal!*"

The laughter grows. Go-Go Girl lifts up his slender legs and laughs out loud. The guy with the Rizzlas shakes with laughter so that he almost drops his hashish but he saves it just in time.

"You don't understand!" I say. "I believe in the power of being an Afrikaner. You people fought for what you believed in, even if it weren't always right. I respect you and your unique language. Because I am English, I feel that I have no roots in Africa. I am almost without history. I wish I were one of you. I ... I like Afrikaners!"

The four of them look at me soberly. Then the poet sighs. He gives me a wry little smile.

"That's a very nice statement, girlie. Now if you go down the passage and turn right, you'll see the kitchen. Get me a beer, hey?"

Grade 12 – *Wynberg Girls' High, Wynberg, Cape*

Denton Isaacs – Battswood Art Centre

The more-green leaf
William Phillips

The more-green leaf
Sailed the winter of grief
Past grim-faced trees
   Of no leaves to hold
Whose bark's left unstripped
   For their dignity sold.

The cursing wind blew ice-cold threats
On the more-green leaf of no regrets
That cast a shadow
   In the shade of the tree
Whose voice was ignored
   But whose body was free.

The grass bent under the winter wind's crown
As the more-green leaf overhead looked down
The blades turned grey
   Shades of green were lost
Their lives it spared
   But their colours it cost.

The wind twisted the clouds with conceited lies
Against the more-green leaf to prove its surmise
That the colour of consent
   Is where no different colours meet
And thus the martyr's journey ends
   By rich-grey bolts of deceit.

The more-green ashes sailed in vain
The selfish winds of no guilty shame
Past trees still grim
   And branches still cold
And grass still grey
   For their dignity sold.

               Grade 11 – *St Stithians College, Randburg*

Though I hear your call ...
Shira Hockman

I travel in a circle drawn on a piece of white paper. A dark graphite line that has been meticulously plotted. Perfectly round, it has been laid out for me and I must walk this relentless path.

In infancy I crawled along the white fibre of life. My naive mind was lost and I was blinded by the bright white light. So society slammed its black boundary around me. It forbade me to frolic nakedly in the light. With a blunt pencil it confined me to a world of secrecy where the whiteness of the light ended in smudged grey on the horizon.

I can see people spinning in their black circles next to mine. They stare blankly into the darkness, dazed with dizziness. Now and again they shift their attention from their frantic manoeuvres to peer into another's circle without understanding.

We do not communicate. We shout and laugh and sing, but the air between us remains silent. The dirty rings consume our merriness. No, we do not communicate.

We show no compassion. We stretch our hands over our unpliable boundaries but our fingers are icy cold. We search into the sightless spirals of each other's eyes; galaxies abound in those black holes, but no one will venture close enough to see and feel. No, we show no compassion either.

My attention is drawn to the dusty horizon. I hear a soft throbbing. Through the haze a faint light glows – there is life there. A man moves freely through the whiteness, he has not allowed himself to be enclosed by those restrictive circles.

I desire his freedom.

There are people around him. They shout and laugh and sing and it echoes through the stale air. Their hands join as they dance together. The warmth flows through them and they share it. Their eyes shine with a calm brilliance. They understand, they communicate, they are compassionate.

I hear their calls, I hear them far away, I hear them break my circle of lifelessness. The thick black rails hang flaccidly.

Suddenly I am struck with terror. The light blinds me. Their sparkling eyes pierce me from all directions. I am frightened without the protection of my circle. I fear those searching eyes, I fear what they will see …

So I scramble back up the rough threads of my broken circle, to where I can conceal myself. I mend the thick black rails, for within them lies my only safety. Here I will remain, spinning in intangible inertia.

I have become a stranger even to myself.

Grade 11 – *King David High, Linden, Jhb*

A moment of terror
Sanjesh Philip

The door creaked. A gust of wind managed to creep in behind Jim Hunter as he entered the room. The fluorescent bulbs above and the shafts of light that filtered into the room did nothing to dispel the gloom that hung in it like morning smog over a city.

At the far end of the room, the familiar figure of Dr Remington, known by everybody as "The Mole", sat hunched behind his desk. His pair of tiny eyes, sandwiched between a thick forehead and fat cheeks, shot up as Jim walked to his place by the window.

"Good morning, Mister Hunter," said The Mole. His smile was cold and his voice crackled like a flame trying to burn wet wood.

Jim muttered a greeting in reply.

Then Jim's colleagues filed in slowly, hesitantly. They had been unusually silent outside and were speaking in whispers. As they walked to their seats they looked nervously at each other and at The Mole. They tried to read his face to find out who would be chosen. The task was not new. They had done similar ones before, but today's was going to be bigger and more complicated than they had ever been asked to perform.

The Mole stood up slowly. He rubbed his fat fingers, cracked his knuckles and his beady little eyes rested on each of them, one by one. They, in turn, tried to make themselves as inconspicuous as possible.

"You have all been briefed on what we are about to do. Today is D-day. Now who will it be?" he asked.

No response.

His hoarse voice crackled once more. His gaze finally rested on Jim. "Right, Mister Hunter, you will be the one. Will you kindly come forward?" he asked.

The rest of the group heaved a unanimous sigh of relief. They had escaped the ordeal. Yet they felt that Jim was the most capable of them all. If anybody could do the job, it was he. He stood up and walked confidently to the front and stood before The Mole.

"This is the big test, son. I hope you're up to it," The Mole whispered. "I want a clean job. Let's not have blood all over the place."

But Jim's confidence was short-lived.

The Mole whipped the plastic cover off the marble slab. Jim's heart sank to his boots and he froze with shock. His eyes grew wide with horror and he went pale.

"Well? Get on with it," ordered The Mole.

Jim shivered as he visualised what lay ahead of him. A chill crept down his spine as though icy fingers had touched him. Bracing himself, he mechanically picked up the razor-sharp instrument. His first move evoked a gasp from his colleagues. He pulled back the head and blood gushed forth. Jim's head began to spin and he was overcome by nausea.

"Come on, Hunter, we are all waiting," said The Mole.

"I ... I ..." The iron fist of fear had gripped Jim's throat and he could not form the words. He tried to continue with the task but his hands felt weak and lifeless.

He gripped the table to restrain himself from throwing up as a wave of nausea overpowered him. The bleeding figure in front of him seemed to turn his big bloodshot eyes towards Jim as if asking:

"Why are you, Jim Hunter, a part of this?"

Jim glanced desperately around the room and through a haze saw the horrified faces of his colleagues. He could vaguely see Dr Remington waving his hands frantically. He tried to focus on the body in front of him. His pulse raced and his heart beat faster and faster. His breath was coming in short gasps.

He couldn't take it any more. He burst out of the room into the morning sunlight and sucked in the cold air. He leaned against a pole, embarrassed but relieved. He stood indecisively for a few minutes, then fled out of the grounds and sprinted down the road. His feet were pounding like pistons as he ran up the pathway to his house. He burst through the front door, past the shocked Mrs Williams carrying a tray, and ran up the stairs to his room.

There, in a corner, sat Joey – contentedly munching on something. The rabbit looked at him with welcoming eyes. He picked it up, petted its fluffy, warm body and hugged it with immense relief.

"I couldn't do it, Joey, I couldn't dissect a rabbit, *no matter what*," he said.

Grade 12 – *Mmabatho High, Mmabatho*

There is an ancient wisdom in Africa, of leaf and soil and season. Look for it.

Donna Ringo
Grade 12 – *King David High, Linden, Jhb*

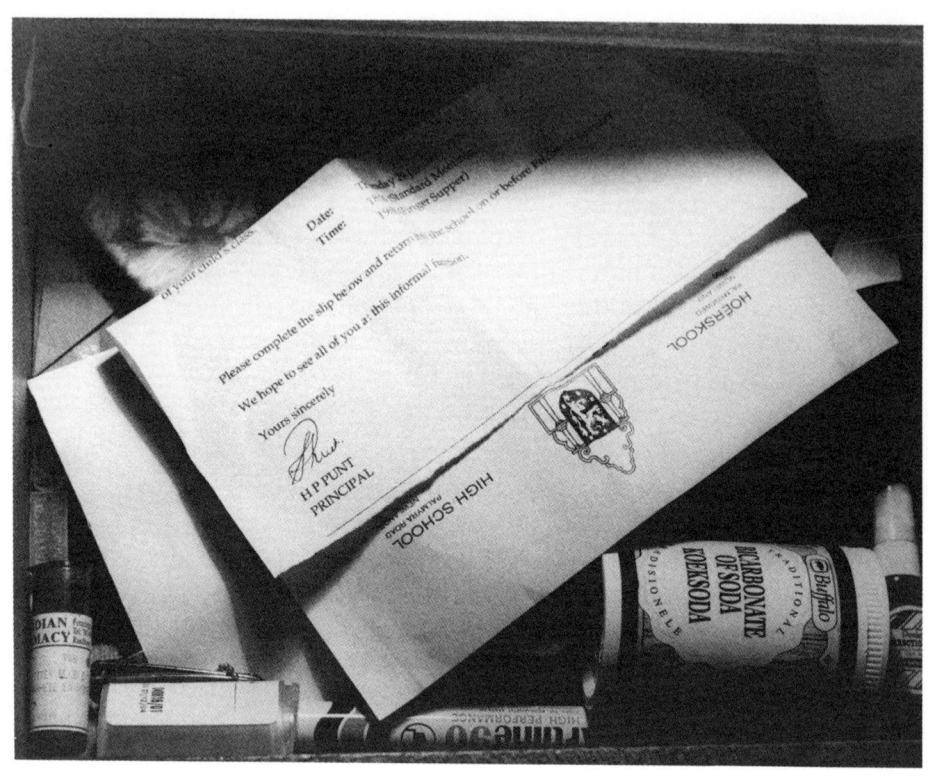

Amelia Kühn – Frank Joubert Art Centre

To risk
Nolusindiso Mali

To laugh is to risk
appearing a fool.
To cry is to risk
appearing sentimental and soft.

To spread your ideas, your dreams
and desires before people,
is to risk
being found boring.

To show strength is to risk
exposing your weakness.
To do is to risk failing,
to live is to risk dying.

But the greatest mistake in life
is to risk nothing.
He who risks nothing,
gains nothing, has nothing, is nothing.
                 Grade 12 – *Khwezi Lomso Comprehensive, Sidwell, PE*

"Summertime and the living is easy"
Graham Thurman

All through winter one thing was on our minds: When would summer come?

Then the first blossoms started appearing and hope was somehow restored. As was peace between feuding parties. For the first time in months we were woken by birds' singing and couldn't help but smile. It was time to say goodbye to heavy winter garments and hello to T-shirts and shorts.

And now exams are over, it's holiday time and we are free at last! Marks do not matter any more and all restraints are kissed goodbye. It's time to meet friends, laugh along with everyone at silly things. Without a care in the world, we stroll out into the night – the boys barely clothed, the girls wearing ever less, with the warm summer winds cuddling them. We stay out all night, sleep under clear skies, with only one thing on our minds: Isn't life great?

The days are filled with swimming and braais, movies and friends, parties and girls. Each day offers an adventure. Simple things please us – like walking along the streets at night through tunnels of oaks. Everything turns out right and not a single thought is wrong. We look at each other and smile; we make all the rules ourselves.

The loyalty of friends, the kindness of the world around us and the beauty of the cool summer nights – we have it all.

It's summertime and the living is easy ...

Grade 11 – *St Stithians College, Randburg*

Top left to bottom right: Andrew Jamieson, Macieck Strychalski, Taariq Nordien, Rupert Jeffries, – Rondebosch Boys' High

Compassion
Clare Matthews

The heaving bundle of paws cowered,
trapped between a fence and my encroaching threat.
Freedom was so close
but the insubstantial barrier was enough to bar the puppy
from lapping up the relief of escape.

It raised pitiful hackles
and bared tiny teeth,
but the facade of that deadly glare
failed to hide the fear
that made its legs quiver.

I knew I could take away that fear,
I could give this puppy a home,
a cosy place to let its body catch up
with its enormous feet.
My heart longed to reach out and love it.

But though I stretched out a gentle hand, it panicked,
turned and squeezed through a small hole in that fence –
a hole not considered before –
for even the smallest hole was enough
to escape all that love.

And as I watched it scampering away,
tumbling over its clumsy paws,
I suddenly realised
how many people I had hurt
when I turned my back on their love.

Grade 12 – *Roedean, Parktown*

In this world of war and suffering, in this world – presented to us as a gift by our Heavenly Father – I find many things that make my heart want to explode with anger and compassion. The Lord sent his own holy Son to us as a gift, but we do not want to accept this gift.

Sello Frangis
Grade 12 – *Marallaneng Senior Sekondêre Skool, Ficksburg*

A handful of rain
Barend Lintvelt

I'll bring you a cupped hand full of rain when you are thirsty for the wonder of wetness.

For then we can hurry on, on our journey of discovery and flee from the jackal and the dust devils. We'll be able to run along forest paths, softly stepping over leaves and twigs. I'll catch you a butterfly and throw it high into the air. The moss and ferns will be soft under our toes. Faster and faster. Leaves slap against our calves. Trees swish by, we tumble and greet the blue sky as we turn.

Moonlight trickles through the leaves, gleaming white on your smooth, naked body as you arch it like a leopard's against the sky. Playful fingers trip over your skin through valleys, planes and hills. Up along your leg and then quickly over your stomach and navel. Your skin quivers like a cat's. I stroke you, up and up and up along the ridges of your spine till my fingers find your hair and my hand brings you closer.

For you, stretched out on a carpet of purple flowers, I bring rain and a kiss in my cupped hand.

Then the wind sweeps us up and we peep behind the sun and into the black holes. Stars sparkle around us and we drink from the Milky Way, slide for a while on Saturn's ring. Then we look further into the craters of the moon for words deeper than "I love you".

We tumble down and the wind plucks at our hair. We land softly on a cloud, it breaks and we eat it like candy floss. Suddenly you push your head through the cloud and pull me along. We fall, fall ... diving, laughing, into the sea.

Bubbles circle up while we sink. Little snails slide by. Angelfish peep and their black-and-white bodies gleam in the half dark. A jellyfish drifts by. Stingrays scare an octopus. We make strings of shells and red corals and hang them around each other's necks.

Then we shoot up and return to the forest. I shake leaves from the autumn trees and softly lay you onto the leafy carpet. Your warm breath caresses my face. Flames shoot through our veins. I smell wild rosemary in your neck. We are entwined. There is no beginning or end. I let myself fall into your depths and find rest in your pale woman-neck.

So I'll bring you a cupped hand full of rain. And you'll sleep in the hollow of my body.

Grade 12 – Hoërskool Calvinia, Calvinia